The Last Mine

The Last Mine: A Post-Apocalyptic Story of Appalachian Resilience

Dale's Story

DK Hall

Author: Derek "DK" Hall

ISBN: 9798329034295

Dedication

This book is dedicated to the people of Appalachia, especially the coal miners. My hometown of Jenkins, KY was one of several coal camp towns built in the area to house more than 24,000 miners in 1912, but the population now barely reaches 2,000.

The coal mining industry has suffered significant decline in recent decades. Once a major coal supplier for the machines that powered industrialization in the US, it has now dwindled to a mere shadow of its former self. Hard working miners, like my father, grandfather, uncles, and many other relatives, risked life and limb to dig the life-blood from beneath the mountains of Eastern Kentucky to help keep the lights on across America.

Your work will not go unrecognized, especially by the children of those men and women who were thankful to see our parents come home each day after their shifts. Thank you for showing us what sacrifice and dedication looked like.

Table Of Contents

Prologue: Dale's Story

Since this is my first attempt at writing, I wanted to provide some character insight. The Last Mine: Dale's Story came about as a tribute to my love for my father, Roger Dale Hall. He worked as a coal miner for nearly 20 years before Beth-Elkhorn closed and left, just six months short of his pension. He was a mine foreman at Mine 25 and was a proud member of the Mine Rescue Team, which achieved great success at national competitions. Despite the hardships of coal mining, which led to him being hospitalized on several occasions, he went to work every day with pride. He instilled in his three sons the values of treating others with respect, helping those who can't help themselves, and putting your heart into everything you do.

A man among men, Pops seemed invincible to us, but he lost his battle with cancer in July 2019 after a valiant fight. He was our hero, and a hero to many, whether he was a coworker, a coach, a city council member, or in one of the various other roles he volunteered for. So, as we approach the fifth anniversary of losing Pops, I wanted to model Dale after the characteristics and personality of Dad, and to veer away from the typical Post-Apocalytic backdrops. I chose to use the very setting he would have prospered in — the coal mines. Pops, you are loved and deeply missed.

~DKH

Chapter 1
Below Ground

Dale slowed his old Dodge pickup as he approached the guard-shack and reached for the volume knob on the cassette player. Gary Stewart, a distant cousin, had been belting out “Drinkin’ Thing”, one of his biggest Country hits, on the tired old Sparkomatic system. Dale had gotten lost in his best rendition as he always loved to sing the bass parts and it helped pass the time on his 45-minute commute to Elkhorn Mine #25. After nearly 20 years of working underground, the grueling work had taken a toll on his body, and he found that a good pre-shift tune seemed to distract him from the aches and pains he would surely add to the tally in the hours ahead. He knew his complaints would fall upon deaf ears, as his brother worked in a nearby mine, just as their father had for many years before them.

“How long are we gonna keep doing this, Dale?,” Eugene asked as he leaned out of the guard-shack window into the frigid February air. "You know we ain't gettin' any younger."

Dale laughed and said, “Eugene, believe me, if there was something better in these mountains when I came back from overseas.... It's all I've really ever known. My pension will be locked-in six months from now, though. Who knows—the boys are all grown and on their own, and I've always wanted a Harley. Be the perfect way to see the open road and go visit 'em."

Eugene nodded in understanding, knowing that Dale had dedicated his life to his family and career. He smiled and said, "You deserve to retire and enjoy life brother, and a Harley sounds like the perfect way to do it. Be safe! You're in the home stretch now!" Eugene pushed the button to raise the gate and turned to the small black and white television set showing Vanna walking towards lit-up tiles, while Pat patiently waited like he did every evening at this time. Dale's tail lights disappeared into the dusty darkness just as Eugene yelled, "SLIGHT OF HAND!!" almost loud enough for Mr. Sajak to hear.

As Dale eased towards the parking lot, his mind couldn't help but transport him to thoughts of Wind Therapy, as his buddies called it, when he could leave this job in the rear-view mirrors and feel the wind in his hair. "Think I'll start checking out the new models this weekend," he said to himself with a grin.

As the old green truck rolled to a stop in the usual parking slot, Dale grabbed his battered black steel lunch pail and his trusty old green Stanley thermos he'd topped off with gas station coffee. He stepped out onto the crunchy snow that remained after the three-inch covering the area had received earlier in the week. It took longer for it to melt in the Appalachian mountains, especially the area surrounding the mines, since the sun only had a short time overhead each day, and the frigid 22-degree temperature didn't help with that process.

Dale shivered and pulled his coat together at the neck and up around his cheeks as he made the short walk to the bathhouse, where the miners could change into their underground gear and could get a shower before they headed home. Fortunately, the temperature in the mine stayed consistently around 60 degrees so there wouldn't be any need to put on more layers to match the cold outside.

After a few minutes of catching up with the guys who had just finished their shift, Dale donned his sticker-adorned mining helmet and made his way to the mine entrance. A low-to-the-ground battery-powered transport vehicle known as a "man trip" was waiting on the night shift crew to take them below ground.

Once the ten-man crew loaded up, they began to make the near-ten-minute trek into the darkness. The men usually kept to themselves during this ride and used the time to reflect on whatever was on their minds or even to ponder how each trip could be their last in this dangerous profession.

In Dale's younger days, he'd been part of the Mine Rescue team, which was utilized more often than anticipated after it was formed several years earlier, due to several tragic collapses in the region. Each mine had its own team, but Dale's had won several competition awards and was one of the best in the country for a three-year stretch. He was very proud of that accomplishment, but after he lost several friends within a short time in situations that were impossible to help them, he decided to pass the torch to some of the younger miners.

Dale had always tried to instill in his three sons to do things the right way, work hard, and respect others until they give you a reason not to. Dale's father Willard worked in the coal mines as well as on the railroads the coal trains hauled their payload across from these deep, dark holes in the ground around the region. Willard was a man's man, who people knew to throw a hundred-pound sack of feed over each shoulder and walk out of the market as easily as a bag boy carrying a box of paper towels. Dale took after his father in many ways and was strong, resilient, and driven in whatever his point of focus was. Those reasons were among the several that made him a well-respected foreman over his crew.

The night shift crew was a good group of workers, as most were newer hires and were eager to learn. Nights weren't for everyone, and Dale had more than done his time on them, but when he was offered a slot as a mine foreman, he had to go back on night shift to fill a vacated slot. He was able to see his sons grow up and move on to their careers, and since he had been divorced for nearly seven years he didn't mind having his nights occupied. As the younger members of the crew boasted about their adventures and their conquests, he just had to laugh and shake his head while he thought back to his own wilder days.

The recent headlines have been dominated by the unstable leadership of North Korea and their hostility towards the United States. They have repeatedly voiced their displeasure that the U.S. refuses to end their occupation of South Korea and they blame our sanctions for their lower standard of living. There have been numerous direct and indirect threats of launching nuclear weapons into the U.S. Capital and strategic cities, with the backing of China, who have also expressed their displeasure with America.

During lunch breaks and water cooler chats, new developments are a hot topic, as the situation has become more serious than anything the night crew has seen in their adult lives. Dale is particularly worried about the decline of coal exports to China, as coal is still used by the U.S. steel industry to supply industrial structures with quality beams and support pieces. China could decide to send warheads to Appalachia, or they could not oppose North Korea doing the same, to stunt industrial growth, which is not typically mentioned in the media.

Normally, the Appalachian population wouldn't worry much about matters of world conflict, but in this case, either country (or both in conjunction) would have the green light to hit the US where it hurts and take out a major player in the steel industry the US depends upon.

The chatter of world headlines just helped break up the shifts and kept each worker wanting to be the one with the breaking news or rumors. You didn't want to come in unprepared and out of the loop. Politics seemed to flare up mostly towards the primaries and nearing November, but most other times it was something that wasn't discussed that much, so as not to cause hard feelings. The most recent developments and rumors, however, have the night shift crew worried, as the latest headlines have indicated that tensions are rising.

Chapter 2 The Devil Knocks

The night shift seemed to drag on, as Dale and his crew repeated their daily tasks almost through muscle memory, although they knew complacency could cause a spark or a misaligned cut into the mountain, either of which could result in disaster. Dale was well aware of this from the post-event studies he did after each disaster his team responded to, so he did his best to engage each of his workers in conversation to keep their minds sharp, and from those talks, he learned the names of the wives and kids of each of his men.

With an hour left in their 12-hour shift, the telephone rang from the foreman's station. There had been no chatter for some time on the headsets each of the miners wore to communicate with one another, which Dale resigned to the crew being lost in thought and ready to head home. In the event communication from the topside was affected by weather or other instances, there was an old-style phone line to serve as the last means of communication. As Dale approached the phone, he keyed his headset a few times to attempt to contact those above ground but only got static. He then realized that most likely was the reason for the phone call, but his mind wondered what could be so pressing to call at 0630 hours, since the crew would be above ground in an hour.

Dale answered the landline, "Let me guess, comms are dow–"

John Green's voice on the other end interrupted him with, "Dale, they've done it. The bastards have nuked us. The news hasn't said if it was North Korea or China or both, but D.C. and the East Coast have been hammered and they keep making their way toward us. Looks like the nukes are causing EMPs too, because the major news outlets from the east coast are off the air. I'm afraid it's only a matter of time before we catch one. Get your guys up here ASAP."

As he felt his stomach drop, Dale answered, "Roger that." and hung up the phone. A few of the workers noticed the expression on his face and removed their headsets as they gathered near him. "I hate to be the bearer of awful news, but it seems that our worst fears have come true. The East Coast, D.C. included, is being hit with a shit-ton of nuclear strikes, which have been followed by EMP effects. John said it looks like they keep making their way inland and it's only a matter of time before we are hit or affected, so we need to get top-side and get to our families." Several of the crew looked like they'd been punched in the gut as they turned and hurriedly gathered their things.

The men, almost in a collective daze, began making their way to the man-trip to head back out of the mine. Hundreds of thoughts went through their heads as they each immediately wondered how they would even begin to survive a nuclear strike. They had each seen "Doomsday prepper" shows and the older movies that showed homes in the '50s and '60s with their varieties of shelters built into the ground or hillsides. Travis "TJ" Johnson settled into his seat and remembered he left his lunch box and other items near his workstation at the conveyor belt. It hit him suddenly that this could be the last time they'd be working in this mine, so maybe it would be best left behind so they can get out of there. Dale ensured everyone was loaded up and told Perry Greer to fire up the transport vehicle and get them to the surface.

Dale's head began to swim with questions of what was happening across the country with the vague information he'd received from John. The overwhelming feeling was that life as he and his men knew it no longer existed. The mantrip suddenly shook violently as the sporadic lighting along the tunnel flickered and then went dark. Perry slowed the buggy, unsure whether to proceed with the poorly designed lighting the buggy was equipped with. The men then shouted "Go, go! Get topside!!" in their different voices and varying degrees of set-in panic since no one wanted to be caught if the roof collapsed. The men began turning on the lights affixed to their hardhats and pointed them ahead of the buggy to help Perry see what was in front of them, as the air in front of the lamps showed clouds of particles in the air from contents sifting through the roof above.

Half of the crew hurriedly got off the buggy and bolted towards the entrance, declaring that they didn't want to get stuck in that hell-hole. Dale made a plea for them to come back, but it went unanswered. As they approached the opening, their silhouettes became visible from the intense brightness they were now facing. Almost in unison, the group of men attempted to shield their eyes with their hands, but they were not prepared for what they were about to witness or how it would affect them. Dale, Perry, Sam, TJ, and Rex decided to increase their distance from the mine opening and ran deeper into the mountain.

A distant rumble quickly got louder, and Dale's last memory of the small group at the entrance was the rush of the anticipated shock front and heat blast he'd read about, which blew the men back into the reinforced mine-opening walls with incredible force. The concussive winds from the shock front continued through the path of least resistance, reaching Dale and his coworkers, launching them further into the infinite darkness of the mine and causing the roof to start collapsing around them.

Dale didn't know how long he was out, but as the cobwebs cleared, he noticed he couldn't move because of what felt like roof timber lying across his back. He felt around in the blackness for his mining helmet light that had apparently come off when he landed. He then remembered the light's battery pack was secured onto his belt, and he could use the line from the battery to the helmet to pull the light to him. Fortunately, it felt like it was free from being caught beneath anything and was quickly back in his hands, where he turned on the lamp with a twist of a knob. The air was cloudy with visible particles from the collapsed roof and splintered support beams, which made it difficult to see much.

After his initial shock, he realized the only way he was getting out of that mine was if he could free himself since it didn't seem as if anyone else had survived from his group. He'd witnessed most of his group being thrown like rag dolls against the mine opening and that it seemed anyone on the surface outside the mine would certainly have been obliterated by the blast and heat.

Dale shined the helmet light towards his pinned body and saw what used to be a portion of the large wooden beam that also had struck Perry, who appeared to be out cold as well. "Perry....PERRY!! Can you hear me??", Dale shouted. He shined his helmet light around his surroundings again in hopes of locating the others. "Rex?? TJ?? Sam??? It's Dale....can any of you hear me??"

After waiting briefly and only hearing the sounds of rocks falling to the ground he knew he had to get himself free. The others had to be in close proximity and were most likely in dire need of help. He couldn't see his legs, so he began a system-check of sorts, starting with his toes on each foot and wiggling them, moving his feet from the ankles, and then attempting to lift his lower legs, but the left one was immobile. He attempted to push up with his right leg and felt pain across his middle and lower back areas from the weight of the large beam. It didn't feel like his lower extremities were in pain, but his left leg was still somewhat trapped.

Dale knew from past experiences with rock falls and roof collapses that so many fellow workers had been trapped and injured, then had to wait on the mine rescue teams to extract them. On this day, mine rescue ceased to exist as Dale once knew it, and he was his own one-man rescue unit. He had suffered numerous injuries in his career that ranged from cuts and bruises to lying in traction in a hospital bed because of his back being struck by large rocks and chunks of ceiling debris, so this was nothing new. He just had to figure out how he could wriggle free.

Dale's physical prowess and determination could prove to be life-saving in such an ominous situation. Despite having given up free weights years earlier, he summoned his God-given strength, stiffened his back, and attempted a push-up to lift the beam and free his trapped leg. Though the excruciating pain was almost unbearable, he persisted in his life or death situation and managed to raise the beam several inches. This enabled him to work his right leg up under his body and beneath the weight of the beam across his back. Undeterred by his painful predicament, Dale utilized his right leg to move the beam back behind him and fortunately freed his left leg. He bent it back and forth a few times to get the circulation flowing, and at the same time also helped to ease his mind that there were no signs of fracture.

After he climbed from beneath the beam, Dale experienced considerable pain across the lower region of his back, where he had previously undergone surgery seven years prior. He surveyed his newly-discovered predicament and reached for his mining helmet and light. He also automatically went to his rear pocket for his cell phone, as it was basically a muscle memory movement in society anymore. Once it came to life, he noticed the screen had been smashed, no doubt during the collapse. Through the fractured glass, he could make out NO SERVICE in the top corner, which made it even more useless. If what happened truly was from a nuclear strike, the cellular networks would now be useless, adding yet another degree of difficulty to getting out of this mine. Nonetheless, he was profoundly grateful to be alive. But, could he be the only survivor?

Chapter 3
Huddling Up

Dust settled over the crumbled cavern, enveloping every surface like a grim veil of darkness. Dale Rogers took a shallow breath, knowing that each gulp of air was precious and should not be wasted. He lay motionless for a moment, his ears filled with the eerie silence that followed the thunderous collapse of the mine.

Ignoring the dull ache in his limbs, he pushed himself up into a sitting position, the beam from his headlamp slicing through the thick haze. His hands skimmed over his body methodically—no searing pain, no gush of warm blood; it seemed he had been spared any serious harm. Relief was a fleeting visitor though, as his thoughts snagged on the welfare of his crew.

"Dale?" The hoarse whisper cut through the stillness. It was Rex, partially pinned beneath a slab of fallen rock, his lanky frame awkwardly twisted.

"Rex, hold on. Try not to move, I'm coming to you," Dale called out, his voice more steady than he felt. He immediately thought back to his years of rescue drills and actual catastrophes as he moved towards his fallen friend.

The rubble around Rex was a chaotic puzzle, but Dale removed stone after stone, revealing Rex's legs. He noticed the older miner wince as he freed one leg, the knee appearing swollen even in the dim light of their headlamps.

"Talk to me, Rex," Dale said as he worked.

"Ah, just my knee." Rex's voice was tight, but his dry humor peeked through. "I've played through worse in my high school days."

"Good to hear," Dale replied, a smile flickering across his face despite the gravity of their situation. Once Rex was free, Dale carefully examined the injured knee. It wasn't a break—that much was clear—but it would slow them down.

"Can you put weight on it?"

"Guess there's only one way to find out." Rex grimaced as he gingerly stood, leaning heavily against the wall of the mine.

"Take it slow," Dale instructed, watching intently as Rex tested his leg. A pained expression flashed across Rex's weathered features, but his knee held.

"Feels like hell, but I can manage," Rex confirmed, adjusting his stance to minimize the discomfort.

"Alright," Dale nodded, his mind already racing ahead. They had to move, to survive, to find the others. The thought of his sons in Kentucky, the family he fought to provide for, galvanized him. His stoic resolve hardened; Dale was not going to let the final chapter of his story end here, not if he had anything to say about it.

"Let's see what we're up against," Dale said, his tone carrying the weight of command. Together, they turned to face the uncertain darkness that lay before them, their headlamps uncovering the the collapsed mine from the darkness that enveloped them.

A mixture of heavy rock and coal dust hovered in the air, and each breath Dale took was an exercise in restraint, as he struggled to fight the urge to cough. His headlamp sliced through the murky darkness, the beam bouncing off jagged rocks and twisted metal that had once been sturdy supports. Rex hobbled alongside him, his tall frame stooped with each careful step.

"Over here," Rex's voice cut through the silence, tinged with both urgency and pain.

Dale followed the sound, stepping gingerly over debris, every muscle tensed for the possibility of causing further collapse. The light revealed TJ first, his back against a wall of coal, eyes wide and breathing shallow. Dale knelt beside him, his hands moving with practiced efficiency over TJ's body, probing for injuries.

"Shoulder," TJ managed to gasp out, his face contorted as Dale's fingers found the source of pain—a dislocated shoulder. "Hurts like a motherf-".

"Rex, brace his back," Dale interjected, interrupting TJ's pain scale descriptor. Rex shuffled closer, providing support with his good leg braced against the ground.

“Where is everybody??’, Perry weakly yelled out to no one in particular.

“Perry?? Where are you?”, Dale inquired.

“How the hell should I know?? I woke up in the dark and can’t find my helmet anywhere. Your voices must have jarred me awake,” Perry said, rubbing the side of his head.

“You ok? Anything broken?” Dale asked.

“Besides a big-assed Flintstone knot on my head, I think I’m alright. I’ll find my way to you. Think I found my helmet and light under a rock that must’ve been the one that KO’d me.”

“AAAAHHH!!! Where am I??”

"Sam??" Dale's voice carried into the darkness beyond TJ.

"Yeah.....I'm here," came a response, weaker than Sam’s usual defiant tone. “What the hell....I dreamed I missed the school bus. Then woke up scratched to pieces.”

They found Sam a few feet away, half-buried under a pile of smaller rocks. Her short-cropped hair was plastered to her forehead with sweat and dust. Cuts laced her arms—shallow but numerous. Dale's hands moved again, quick and sure, sweeping the debris from her legs before helping her to sit up.

"Anything broken?" he asked, scanning her for more serious injuries.

"Feels like it's just cuts and bruises," Sam replied, gritting her teeth as she flexed her fingers.

"What about the others? This is only half the crew," TJ asked, grimacing and holding his shoulder.

"Dale answered him with a simple shake of his head. "We need to move. Let's try to make a path," Dale said, turning his attention to the collapsed roof that sealed them in.

Together, they approached the rubble that blocked their once familiar exit, now a tomb of stone and timber. Dale reached out, his fingers tracing the cold rock, searching for any sign of weakness, any crack that might give them hope. But the gap between life and entrapment was sealed tight, the stones packed together as if nature herself had conspired to keep them caged.

Dale pressed his ear to the cold, hard surface of rock that had sealed them in, his breath shallow as he listened for signs of life beyond the barrier. "Can anyone hear us?" Beside him, the others joined in, their voices a desperate chorus stalling at the immovable barrier and going no further. Several of them took turns banging rocks against the newly formed barrier in hopes someone would hear.

"Hello? Is anybody out there?" Sam's voice cracked with exertion, her words fading without reply. TJ tried to add his voice, but pain twisted his features into a grimace as he cradled his injured shoulder.

Minutes dragged like hours, the silence from the outside world becoming its own presence among them—a heavy shroud of abandonment. No echoes returned, no hopeful taps or calls, just the eerie stillness of the mine.

"Nothing," Dale said. As the reality of their situation was sinking in, the hopelessness of their circumstances becoming more apparent with each passing moment. As they stood there in silence, the only sound was the smaller tumbling rocks as they broke free from above, a stark reminder of their solitude.

"Careful," Rex warned, noticing a precarious stack of debris that looked ready to shift with the slightest provocation.

"Doesn't look good," Dale muttered, the edge in his voice betraying his concern. He stepped back, surveying the damage, aware that even the vibrations of their voices could beckon another deadly shift.

"Let's not waste energy here," he decided after a moment heavy with unspoken fears. "We need to huddle up and get a plan; gotta be smart about this."

"Looks like we're on our own, at least for now," Sam said, brushing the dirt from her arms, her voice attempting to sound brave.

"Could be worse," TJ offered weakly, trying to find comfort in the camaraderie that had always bound the crew together.

"It can always be worse, brother," Dale agreed, though his eyes, ever assessing, told a different story—one where the possibilities of suffocation and starvation loomed as real threats within these confined walls. "My cellphone got crushed, but I could still make out 'no service' in the upper corner. Could just be inside here, but you guys might want to check yours."

Perry confirmed, "No service on mine.", as Sam and TJ both shook their heads and crammed the useless technology back into their cover-alls.

"Alright," Dale said finally, his voice the anchor in the dark. "We'll push towards the supplies and medical gear. That's our best shot. Let's get moving. We aren't going to be in good air for long."

"Lead the way," Rex said, the years of trust between them as solid as the earth that surrounded them. "And we really need to think about air. We're burning it with every word. Let's keep it to a minimum unless it's something urgent."

"Right," Dale nodded, his mind switching gears, the instincts honed from years underground kicking in. He scanned the faces of his crew, each one etched with the stark reality of their predicament. "We need to check if we're boxed in."

Together, they moved with purpose, their headlamps casting eerie shadows on the walls as they navigated the confined space toward the mine's interior. The air felt different here—stale and reluctant to move. It whispered warnings of oxygen growing thin.

"Feels tight back here," Rex observed, running his fingers along a jagged crack in the wall where dust drifted lazily down. "But we can't be certain without checking further."

"Let's hope we have a way out behind us," Dale said, his thoughts turning to the grim alternative. They pushed on, fatigue setting in, until they reached what was left of a junction. Here, the collapse had not been so complete. A small mercy.

"Look," Dale pointed to the narrow gap overhead where the dim glow of their lamps revealed less devastation. "It's bad, but it's not a full cave-in. We can get through this."

"Then that's where we focus our energy," Rex agreed, the lanky frame of his body already assessing the blockade before them.

“We should limit the lights to one at a time, two at the most. These batteries won’t last forever and without them, we are screwed,” Perry added.

"Agreed. Conservation is key," Dale added, picturing the faces of his sons, the lives waiting for him beyond these suffocating walls. "We dig smart, we dig together. We work in shifts, keep the noise down, and watch for signs of bad air. We'll take breaks, make every movement count.”

"Got it, boss," Sam replied, determination in her eyes.

"Let's move some mountains, literally," TJ quipped, despite the throb in his shoulder.

They set to work carving a path through the chaos, each scrape of stone against stone a testament to their unyielding defiance.

Dale's fingers traced the jagged edges of fractured stone, assessing the damage behind them. An entanglement of debris had sealed their fate, but in its midst, an opportunity presented itself. "Why not use the straps on the mantrip and move the bigger rocks out of the way? If we clear a path wide enough, we can use the buggy to get as far as possible instead of all of us struggling to breathe making our way deeper into the mine."

"Good call. Better to clear this out," he said, pointing toward the twisted maze that once was a passageway. "We've got supplies waiting on the other side." His voice carried the weight of their predicament, each word etched with the gravity of their situation.

Rex nodded, his gray hair dusted with pulverized rock. They grabbed the mantrip's ratchet straps, sturdy as the mountains themselves, and began the laborious task of clearing a path a bit wider than the buggy. Muscles strained against the stubborn resistance of stone and timber, the air thick with the gritty scent of disturbed earth.

Sam, ever the fighter, took to reinforcing the compromised areas with whatever materials they could repurpose. She wedged broken timbers at precarious angles, her tattooed arms flexing under the strain. Each thud of wood against rock was a defiant blow that increased their odds of survival.

"Keep it steady," Dale instructed, watching as TJ winced with every movement. "Slow and deliberate, conserve your strength."

After a while, which felt like time standing still in their new environment, the group paused, fatigue etched in the lines of their faces. They knew the stakes; they felt the void filled with silence beyond the collapse, a reminder of their isolation. They had forged a path wide enough for the mantrip to get past the collapsed area around them and make their way to their supplies and first aid kit.

"Let's split up," Dale decided after a moment, his gaze lingering on the blocked entrance where hope might yet flicker. "Sam, TJ, you stay here. Keep trying to make contact. Rex, Perry, you're with me. We ride the mantrip as far as we can, then hoof it the rest of the way if we have to."

Perry grunted an acknowledgment, the Marine in him coming to the fore, ready for the mission at hand. Together, they climbed aboard the old four-wheeled buggy - a relic that had somehow survived the devastation. Its metal frame rattled loudly as they set off.

"Stay sharp," Dale warned, as Perry engaged the forward gear of the mantrip, creating a low hum that reverberated through the tight and enclosed space. The group advanced, with the headlights of the buggy cutting through the darkness and illuminating their path. They encountered obstacles which they tackled with unwavering determination, using ratchet straps to pull and exerting themselves until they cleared the way towards safety.

With that, they plunged deeper into the remnants of their world, their hard work a testament to their resolve. They were miners, and surrender was not etched into their bones.

Dale defiantly stepped through the debris The angled walls were illuminated by the flickering glow of his headlamp, casting dancing shadows as Perry and Rex followed closely behind, their breath visible in the cool air as they navigated the final treacherous half-mile on foot.

"Watch your step," Dale cautioned over his shoulder, his voice carrying the weight of responsibility. They climbed over debris and rugged terrain, a vivid reminder of the mountain's immense power.

"Supply station's just up ahead," Rex announced, his depth of experience reading the mine's layout like a well-worn map etched into his mind.

When they finally reached the last station, the sight of it was like beholding an oasis amidst the devastation. Oxygen tanks stood in orderly rows, reflecting the beam of Dale's lamp with a sheen of hope. Perry wasted no time snagging medical kits, while Dale gathered pre-packed MRE-type food packs and bottles of water.

"Rex, you sure you're good here?" Dale asked, eyeing the older man who was already assessing the supplies with the acumen of a seasoned miner.

"Go take care of Sam and TJ, I've got this," Rex replied, his gaze not leaving the cache as he inventoried the resources with meticulous care. "Take a couple of O2 tanks with you too. You might need to get a puff off of them here and there, as well as our folks up front."

Their arms full, Dale and Perry retraced their steps to the mantrip, then navigated the wreckage back to where Sam and TJ awaited aid. The return journey was marked by their ominous silence, broken only by the hum of the buggy and the distant, hollow drips of water somewhere deep in the bowels of the earth.

Arriving back at the collapsed entrance, they found Sam leaning against the wall, her face drawn tight with pain, while TJ sat grimacing, clutching his shoulder in quiet agony. Perry immediately knelt beside them, his movements precise as he administered first aid. Ace bandages were wrapped, antiseptic applied, and pain dulled with what little medication they had.

"Any luck reaching the outside?" Dale asked, once the immediate needs were met.

"Nothing," Sam replied, her voice hoarse. "It's like we're ghosts down here."

"Let's get you both fueled up," Dale said, passing out rations of food and water, the simple act of sharing a meal offering a semblance of normalcy in the chaos.

Finished with their tasks, the group crowded into the mantrip, its motor humming to life once more for the journey back to Rex.

The mantrip came to a halt, and they disembarked, the reunion brief and wordless, their expressions conveying all that needed to be said. They arrived to find Rex perched on a crate, finishing up a swig of fresh O2, his figure a solitary sentinel among the stockpile.

"Alright, let's regroup," Dale began, his mind already turning over their options. "We've got supplies, but we're still trapped. We need to think about the air, about finding a way out."

The others nodded, their faces set with the same determination that had carried them this far. They gathered around a helmet light Rex had repurposed to be a lamp hanging above the work station desk. These were five miners bound by blood forged deeper than the coal seams they worked, ready to face whatever lay ahead.

Chapter 4
Digging Out

Dale's breath came in shallow gasps, the heavy air in the mine pressing down on him like a physical weight. He could see the same strain mirrored in the faces of his crew, their eyes wide with the dawning realization that the oxygen was running thin. Panic fluttered in his chest, but he clamped down on it hard. Years of leading men through earth's dark caverns had taught him the cost of yielding to fear.

"Listen up," Dale's voice cut through the thick silence, steady despite the desire to survive coursing through his veins. His weathered face, usually stoic and unreadable, betrayed a flicker of urgency. "We're running low on air. We need to find a way out, and fast. We have several tanks, but we need to use those as a last resort. Hopefully it won't come to that. Our lights aren't going to last much longer either.

The haunting glow of the lone helmet light cast long shadows as the group gathered around in a tight circle. Dale saw more than just fear in their determined gazes; he saw the rugged tenacity that life in the Appalachian Mountains had etched into their very bones.

"Any ideas?" he asked, his voice rough as gravel. The question hung in the stale air, a challenge to the conditions that sought to claim them.

"We could try digging out by hand," offered one, a grim set to his mouth.

"Too slow. And we risk bringing down more of the loose rock on us," countered another quickly.

"Then what about using the equipment?" A younger voice piped up, tinged with both apprehension and hope.

"Most of it's trapped under the rubble," Dale replied, but his mind raced, turning over every possibility with the precision of a man who had spent half his life coaxing secrets from the unforgiving earth.

"Wait..." Dale's gaze fixed on the mantrip—their ride into the mine and potential lifeline out. It wasn't much, but it was something. "The big battery on the mantrip still holds charge. If we can rig it to power any of the drills, even for a short time..."

A murmur of cautious optimism rippled through the group. Dale watched as the spark of an idea took hold, igniting a flame that pierced the encroaching despair. They were miners, after all, who bent the very rock to their will.

"We need to inspect what's left of the gear. Anything that can help us break through, we use it," Dale declared, his voice resonating with a commander's authority.

In the dim light, their movements were swift and deliberate, each one knowing their role. There was no room for error—not when their lives hung on the edge. Every second and every breath counted. Dale led them, his thoughts flickering to the sons he had raised to be strong and resourceful, the family he had left behind thousands of times in pursuit of a day's honest work. He would not let this mine become his grave.

As they huddled around the remnants of their tools of trade, a new chapter in their struggle for survival began to unfold. Their plan was filled with uncertainty, but beneath the surface lay the unyielding spirit of a generation that refused to go gently into the night.

Dale's gaze settled on Rex, whose silhouette was etched against the backdrop of twisted metal and broken machinery. The older miner stepped forward, his shadow long in the flickering light from the headlamp.

"Listen up," Rex's voice cut through the murmur of anxious breaths and shifting feet. "We break down one of these drills, strip it to the bones. It'll make a hole through the mess."

Skepticism clouded the faces around him, but Rex stood unshaken—a monolith amidst the chaos. Dale watched as doubt vied with hope in the eyes of his crew. They had seen drills fail, steel bend, rock refuse to yield. Yet there was something in Rex's steady tone, the set of his jaw, that quelled the rising tide of panic.

"Rex, those drills weren't meant for this kind of job," one miner objected, his voice echoing off the close walls.

"Neither were we," Rex shot back, a wry smile cutting across his face. "But here we are."

Without waiting for consent, Rex bent over the chosen drill. His hands moved with practiced ease, stripping away unnecessary parts, trimming it down to its core. With each piece removed, Dale felt the weight of their plight lessen ever so slightly.

"Help me with these," Rex called out, nodding toward an assortment of scrapped materials. Together, they rigged makeshift wheels beneath the pared-down behemoth. The contraption was crude, but functional—a tribute to Rex's four decades spent mastering the guts of the earth.

"Let's move," Dale said, his voice a low command.

They grunted with exertion as they maneuvered the drill through the dark tunnels. Their muscles ached and protested as they heaved the machine over fallen beams and jagged rocks. Sweat mixed with coal dust on their skin, streaking them with black.

"Careful!" someone shouted as the drill teetered close to a pit of darkness. They strained their arms and righted it, continuing onward.

"Keep it steady," Dale urged. Their progress was choppy, cadenced by obstacles that threatened to thwart them. But with every inch gained, the mine's grip loosened, bringing them closer to open air and survival.

"Almost there," Rex panted, his gray hair drenched with sweat. His humor might be dry, but his resolve was anything but.

Dale nodded, sharing a look with Rex that spoke of shared burdens and unspoken fears. This was their life and always had been. A battle against the earth that gave as much as it took. Now, it was a fight not just for coal, but for breath, for light, for life itself.

The drill, now a beacon of their resolve, was wrestled into position behind the mantrip for its journey. Dale's hands, roughened by a lifetime of labor, guided the heavy equipment with a precision that belied his urgency. The group worked in tandem, their movements deliberate and measured, as if the wrong move could shatter the fragile thread of hope they clung to.

“Here goes nothin’,” Perry said in almost a whispered tone as he eased the mantrip forward. “Keep an eye on it, and I’ll try to hold it steady through the gauntlet.” For ten grueling minutes, the buggy eased over the remaining chunks of rock and splintered beams that formerly were overhead, but finally the group had the ominous hindrance to the outside world in the headlights of the mantrip.

"Easy does it," Dale cautioned, his eyes scanning the complex mechanism before them. They had to secure the drill in such a way that it wouldn't jostle free during operation; this wasn't just machinery anymore—it was their lifeline.

"Strap it down good," Rex directed, his knowledge of the equipment shining like a lamp in the murk. With skillful hands, he showed them how to use the belts from the mantrip to lash the drill firmly to its frame. The thick belts cinched tight, holding the ungainly bulk tighter than a toddler in a carseat.

"Trust me, boys. She won't budge an inch," Rex asserted, and Dale noted the faintest quiver of emotion in his otherwise steady voice. It wasn't fear—Rex didn't know how to fear—but rather the weight of responsibility for every life in this dark chamber.

The silence hung heavy as Rex paused, pulling a rag from his pocket to wipe away the fresh sheen on his brow. Then, with a nod towards the mantrip, he set to work on the electric motor. The others watched, muscles tensed, ready to jump in or dash out, whichever the moment called for.

With nimble fingers, Rex rerouted wires, his face illuminated intermittently by the spark of connections being made. A hush fell upon the group, punctuated only by the sound of metal against stone and the occasional crackle of electricity.

"Give 'er some juice," Rex finally said, stepping back from the mantrip.

Dale hesitated, took a deep breath, then threw the switch. There was a moment of nothing—a stretched second where doubt could have crept in—and then the drill roared to life. Its vibrations thrummed through the ground, up their legs, and into their chests, a mechanical heartbeat that fueled their pulse with renewed vigor.

"Hot damn!" one of the younger miners exclaimed, the words slicing through the drone of the machine.

"Quiet!" Dale snapped, more out of reflex than reprimand. They couldn't afford carelessness, not when success balanced on a knife's edge.

But the sternness in his voice couldn't mask the upward twitch of his lips, nor the light that sparked in eyes dulled by too many hours in the dark. They all felt it—a surge of excitement so potent it bordered on euphoria, the possibility of escape suddenly tangible, vibrating along with the drill in the cramped space of the mine.

"Steady, baby," Rex murmured, placing a hand on the vibrating metal as if feeling for the pulse of the earth itself. "This ain't over yet."

And though the air remained thick with dust and fear, and the danger of their situation pressed close, in that moment there was room to breathe. Room to dream of open skies and the chance to hold out hope for seeing their families once again. Room, at last, for hope.

Dale watched as the makeshift assembly of man and machine became a lifeline. The drill, once just another instrument for extracting coal, was now their sole chance at deliverance. TJ's hands gripped the controls first, his lean frame rigid with concentration. His youth and bum shoulder did little to betray his resolve. Each turn seemed to demand more from him than mere physical strength..

"Keep it steady," Dale instructed, his voice cutting through the strained silence. He remained close, eyes tracking every movement, every shift of debris that signaled both progress and doom.

Samantha "Sam" Thompson took over next, her muscles flexing under inked skin, a silent testament to her readiness to fight. She pushed the drill forward with a force that belied her size, her jaw set in fierce determination. Each rotation of the drill bit tore through the obstruction with a promise of freedom.

"Watch that torque, Sam," Rex warned, his years of expertise lending authority to his words. The tension in his lined face spoke volumes as he observed the precarious operation—a single misstep could bury them all. Sam's return expression let Rex know that she wouldn't be the one to let their chances falter.

Perry Greer swapped in, high-and-tight hair glistening with sweat. The ex-Marine moved with precision, applying his training to the rhythm of the machinery, every action measured and purposeful. Despite their differences, Rex nodded in approval, the playful banter between them lost to the gravity of their task.

"Good job, Marine. Keep her going," Rex said, his dry humor replaced by an uncharacteristic note of encouragement.

A dull gleam caught Dale's eye, a pinprick of light that expanded with each push of the drill. It was the outside world, piercing their underground tomb. Cautious optimism sparked among the crew, flickering across weary faces like the first break of dawn.

"Look," Sam murmured, her wiry frame leaning in to catch a glimpse of the light. "We're breaking through."

"Easy... easy," Dale soothed, his hand steadying TJ's shoulder as he resumed control. They were miners, accustomed to the earth's dark embrace, but this light —it was different. It was salvation.

"Can you believe it?" Sam breathed out, her voice a mixture of hope and disbelief.

"Let's not count our blessings just yet," Dale replied, though his heart hammered with the same cautious elation. They had made it this far on grit and shared resolve, but the sight of daylight promised more than escape—it whispered of life beyond the rubble.

"Keep it straight! We're almost there!" Dale commanded, his own hands itching to take the controls. But this was a collective struggle, their success hinged on unity.

And then, without warning, the resistance gave way, and a shaft of light poured into their subterranean cage. The beam cut through the dust motes dancing in its path, casting long shadows against the walls of coal.

"Fresh air," someone gasped, and they all paused to savor the sweet influx of oxygen that accompanied the light.

Chapter 5
The World We Know

"Alright, let's not get distracted. Secure the hole and make sure it's stable," Dale ordered, pulling them back to reality. There was no room for error—not when so much was at stake.

They exchanged looks of silent understanding, each one aware that the hardest part was yet to come. But for now, they allowed themselves that brief moment of respite, of tentative joy in the face of a world waiting to be rediscovered.

Dale's hand trembled on the drill controls, his eyes fixed on the thin beam of light that was their lifeline. The machine groaned a final time before the wall of debris buckled, and an audible rush filled the cavern as air from the outside world spilled into the mine's stale corridors. It carried with it the scent of pine and earth, with a pungent undertone that made Dale's nose wrinkle.

"Steady," he cautioned, his voice barely rising above the sound of their new atmosphere invading old spaces. "Take it slow."

One by one, they approached the breach, their breaths shallow and deliberate. They were cautious, knowing too well the danger of hope's intoxication. Dust swirled in the influx of daylight, particles dancing like tiny specters in the grayish beam that broke through the darkness. They watched in silence, transfixed by the simple beauty of dust motes set ablaze by the sun—freedom's first ambassadors.

"Let's get those masks from the buggy and move out," Dale finally said, nodding toward the opening.

Climbing through the hole, they emerged one by one into a world draped in silence. Dale was the last to step out, his boots crunching on a carpet of fallout that muted the landscape. He stood there, a figure carved from the very mines he had toiled in for decades, now facing the aftermath of mankind's foolishness.

The sight that greeted them was a lament in itself—the once-vibrant Appalachians lay in ruin, stripped of their greenery, the trees skeletal against a heavy gray sky. In the distance, where homes had once dotted the slopes like patchwork, there was only devastation. The mountains, resilient through ages, bore the scars of a war that had not honored their majesty.

Dale's heart sank as the reality set in; there would be no homecoming, no reunions. His thoughts turned involuntarily to his sons, to the people who had been part of his every day. Had they felt anything in their final moments? Or had life slipped away as suddenly as these mountains had been defaced?

"God help us," murmured a voice beside him, echoing the hollow ache in Dale's chest.

He turned to his crew, men and women who looked to him for guidance, their faces etched with grief and shock. But beneath that, a resilience flickered—the same stubborn resolve that had seen them through the bowels of the earth.

"Let's gather what we can," Dale said, his voice steady despite the turmoil within. "We survive. That's what we do. For them, for those who aren't here to fight anymore."

They nodded, a silent pact forming between them, unity forged in loss. And as they set to work amid the remnants of their world, Dale knew this was more than survival; it was a tribute to those they'd lost, a declaration that even in the face of desolation, the human spirit endures.

Soot and ash drifted through the remnants of what once had been the sturdy gatehouse, now standing crooked, a sentinel to ruin. Dale navigated over the debris that carpeted the ground as he scanned their surroundings—the mine property was a graveyard of vehicles and buildings, some half-collapsed, others scorched beyond recognition.

"Check for food, water, medical supplies—anything that might still be useful," Dale commanded, his voice cutting through the eerie silence that enveloped the group. The miners dispersed with urgency in their steps, each movement deliberate, knowing now that the very mine they escaped from offered the only semblance of safety in this desolate new world.

They rummaged through the debris, salvaging cans of beans from the canteen, cases of water from the administrative offices, and first aid kits from the safety station. Each find was a small victory against the overwhelming odds they faced.

"Found some spare light batteries!" someone called out, holding up their treasure like a prized relic of the past.

"Bring 'em here," Dale replied, directing them towards a pile of gathered goods in a warped wheel barrow he'd stumbled across.

One thing we haven't found...I don't even want to say it," TJ said with a solemn tone. His eyes darted around the ash-covered property in an attempt to disprove his efforts.

"I was thinkin' the same thing, TJ," Sam added, with marked sadness in her voice.

"I doubt we'll find any of our mining family, gang. What I saw right before I blacked out...I don't know how any of what's here is still in front of us," Dale said, recalling the moment the mine went from the darkest dark to the most brilliant light he could have ever imagined. "It hit us danger-close. That mine was all that saved us. Maybe a ways off from us might have had less devastation, but we soaked up the brunt of it," he added. "It wasn't an accident this area was hit so hard."

"Yeah," Perry added, "from the outside lookin' in, the coal we pull outta Mother Earth helps make the steel to throw up all those new big-city plants and office buildings. Guess they got tired of us kickin' their tail at bein' awesome and tried to hit us where it would hurt the whole country."

Nods of affirmation from the group followed Perry's statement. The silence that followed was the realization that what they came to work to do each night had much more significance than just keeping the lights on, as so many bumper stickers in the area proclaimed.

"Let's get back to it, gang," Dale said, in an attempt to break the silence. "We need to wrap it up for today and get back inside, away from who knows what's floatin' around us. Looks like that big old hole in the mountain we've all cursed at times might just be our saving grace. But we have some work to do," Dale said after they had collected what they could. His eyes lingered on the horizon, where the sky met the jagged silhouette of the mountains—a stark reminder of the world they were leaving behind.

As they continued to work, the reality of their circumstances pressed in around them. They were miners, not scavengers—but necessity had made them both.

Once they arrived back at the entrance they'd drilled, Dale knelt down, examining the edges of the hole. They needed a barrier to keep the contaminated air out. A storage room in one of the remaining block office buildings had several large pieces of insulation, which they could affix to the entrance to filter out the air, and seal the rest of the opening with rags, plastic sheeting, and anything else they could layer.

"Hand me that duct tape," he instructed, taking the silver roll from one of the crew. With unmatched determination, he began securing the makeshift materials around the perimeter of the hole, creating a rudimentary seal.

"Think it will hold?" asked Sam, her voice tinged with the fear all of them felt but none dared speak aloud.

"It'll have to," Dale responded without looking up, focusing on the task. "We'll reinforce it as we find better materials. It should at least keep the bad air out, the good air in. I'll poke holes in each side of the insulation to let it filter what does come through. It's not perfect, but it's what we've got."

The rest of the crew joined in, working alongside Dale, their faces set in grim determination. They layered, taped, and fortified, each action a testament to their will to survive in the face of an uncertain future.

"Good work," Dale finally said, stepping back to inspect their handiwork. "Let's head in. We've got a lot to do if we're going to make this place livable."

As they retreated into the darkness of the mine, the light from outside dimming as the filter took hold, Dale couldn't help but think of his sons, his former wife, the life he'd known. With no time to waste, they couldn't afford to ponder over what might have been lost. Instead, they had to swiftly shift their focus and adapt to the unfamiliar territory they found themselves in. The ominous abyss that surrounded them was filled with dangers, and they needed to be extremely cautious to avoid any potential harm. Despite the looming threats, they searched for comfort amidst the darkness, hoping to find solace in this strange and foreboding place.

"Alright, let's take stock of what we've got," Dale's voice cut through the silence, gruff but steady. He knelt by the pile of supplies they'd scavenged, his fingers deftly sorting through the cans of food, bottles of water, and assorted tools.

TJ crouched beside him, his youthful face drawn tight with concern under the flickering light. "I never thought I'd be callin' this place home," he muttered, the edge of his Southern drawl frayed with fatigue.

"None of us did," Sam interjected, her tattooed arms folded as she leaned against the cool rock wall. Her glare pierced the shadows, fierce and unwavering.

Rex, leaning on a rusted pickaxe, nodded solemnly. "Our forefathers survived awful times in these mountains. We'll honor them by doing the same."

Perry huffed a laugh, though it lacked humor. "Well I sure don't feel like a pioneer at the moment."

A silence descended upon the group, each lost in their own thoughts as the gravity of their situation settled like coal dust in their lungs. The outside world was a wasteland—radiation, the inevitable spool-up of raider groups, and the relentless march of time all conspiring against them. Yet here they were, bound together by circumstance and necessity, a disparate band of survivors clinging to the hope of another sunrise.

Dale stood, stretching his aching back, feeling every one of his years in the protest of his muscles. "We've been through hell today," he said, his gaze sweeping across the faces of his crew. "But we're still here, still breathing. We're going to make it through this, together."

"Damn straight," Perry said, clapping a hand on Rex's shoulder.

"Let's set up shifts for watch," Dale continued, slipping into the role of leader as naturally as breathing. "We need to stay alert. Who knows if there are others out there trying to find somewhere to crash. I vote we each find a place to curl up and try to get some rest. And tomorrow, we start workin' on making this place more than just livable. For the foreseeable future, we have to make it our home.

As the group dispersed, Dale remained standing for a moment longer, staring into the darkness that stretched before them. The uncertainty of their future loomed large, a monstrous thing that threatened to swallow them whole. With that, Dale turned away from the blackness and walked toward the flickering headlamps of their encampment, ready to face whatever lay ahead.

Chapter 6
Beyond the Comfort Zone

The imperfect covering they'd formed over the mine opening allowed subdued morning daylight to cut a swath through the murky darkness of the mine, revealing the grim determination etched into the faces of his vaguely rested crew. They huddled together in the cavernous belly of the earth, their collective breaths now the life force of this once-thriving industrial womb. Dust motes danced in the beams of their lights as they surveyed the remnants of their previous day's toil now transformed into a survival cache.

Dale stood and cleared his throat in the middle of the group. "Mornin' everyone. Hopefully, everyone was able to rest somewhat. I know it was hard for me to close my eyes and not think about loved ones and a hundred other things. During my watch, I could hear the heartbreak among everyone, mine included," Dale empathetically revealed in a much more somber tone than he normally used as a leader. "We are all the family we have as far as we know, until we find out otherwise, and I have prayed hard that each of us has good news down the road at some point."

“That being said, I’ve sure thought a lot about our situation here, and feel free to chime in if anyone has a better idea or objects to something. First off, access to good air is gonna be our lifeline," Dale declared, his voice echoing against the stone walls. "We’ll need a better filter system, something makeshift but effective. Something better than insulation with holes poked in it. Also, as far as a livin’ area, the section of the mine we are in will be our best bet because of the air quality. The work station would be great since it’s bigger and has most of our supplies, but with no electric to power the fans to get the air flowin’, we all know it’s a death trap waiting to happen. I feel like we can fortify the area around us to be a safe haven—a bunker of sorts— and expand back into the mine as we are able. We can keep supplies back in the work station, using it as a storage area that would be out of harm’s way, especially if the mine is breached by unwanted guests while we are out gathering what we can. I think a few of us should head back to the work station to start the day off and grab what we need to start covering the opening into our bunker, then see what else we need to make or find to make that happen."

Nods of agreement bobbed around him, and the crew scattered without further command, already familiar with the layout of their subterranean refuge. They scavenged through the remnants of their previous lives: mesh screens once used for sifting coal, rolls of duct tape that could seal any breach, and spare cloths that might serve a new vital purpose. Their movements were methodical, each step taken with the slow, deliberate pacing of those who understood that every action now carried weight beyond measure.

Perry, with his high-and-tight hair still managing to look orderly even under these circumstances, returned from the depths clutching a spool of copper wire. He laid out his treasure trove on a tattered tarp as if presenting an offering to the gods of survival. “Copper thieves must have missed this one. We had about a dozen spools taken a couple of months ago. Can’t leave anything outside unattended or that isn’t bolted down. Hell, they’ll steal the bolts, too.”

"EMP wouldn't have fried everything," Perry started, his words punctuated by the rip of tape as they pieced together their creation. "Older model vehicles—before the computers took over—they'll run. If we can get one going, mobility means we can scout for more supplies, get a real lay of the land."

Dale paused, considering Perry's proposition. The man was right; an operational vehicle could change the game entirely. And there was something about the possibility that sparked a glimmer in Dale's chest—a faint echo of hope amidst the devastation.

"My old Dodge truck is in the employee lot," Dale mused, more to himself than to Perry. "Battery might be toast, but she's sturdy. No fancy electronics to speak of. And during our walk yesterday, it looked as if she'd fared better than some of the others."

"Let's give it a shot then," Perry replied, the Marine in him rising to the challenge. "Could be our ticket outta this place when the time comes. I'll go with you since there may be lurkers out and about looking for what they can salvage, and a running vehicle will be top priority these days."

The group optimistically nodded their heads almost in unison at the potential boost to their survival chances.

Dale and Perry shared a silent understanding, the generational gap between them sealed shut by the urgency of their mission. They secured the last piece of mesh onto the makeshift air filtration frame with a final strip of tape, standing back to admire their handiwork. After a quick once-over, Dale said, "I think that will do for what materials we have. Definitely better than our first attempt."

"Alright, let's go before darkness sets in and see if that old beast has any life left in her," Dale said, his voice carrying a hint of the same resilience that had seen him through dark days beneath the earth and in foreign lands alike.

With that, they shouldered their tools and turned toward the ascent, their headlamps piercing the oppressive blackness, ready to confront whatever awaited them in the ghostly remains of a world lost to ash and echoes.

The mantrip's wheels rolled over the gritty floor, the sound muffled by the walls of the mine as TJ and Sam led Dale and Perry back through the tunnels. corridor was a testament to years spent navigating the subterranean darkness, yet now, absent were the familiar echoes of the crew's banter and the hum of machinery. Only the buggy's headlamps cut through the blackness, casting long shadows that danced with every movement.

"Feels like we are cruising through a crypt," Perry murmured, his voice low, almost swallowed by the hum of the motor that enveloped them.

"Keep watching for loose rocks," Dale replied, the miner in him refusing to yield to the disturbing atmosphere, clinging instead to the practicalities of survival.

They emerged into what once was daylight; a sickly glow filtered through a haze of suspended ash, painting the world in monochrome. The landscape lay barren before them, older buildings crumbled like the carcass of civilization, its bones picked clean by the vultures of war.

"Lord almighty," Perry exhaled, taking in the devastation. "I'll never get used to this. Better mask up. Heaven only knows what's in this air, and we definitely can't afford to get sick."

"Let's just get to the truck," Dale said as he pulled his N95 mask from his backpack, his voice a fortress against despair, though his eyes betrayed the ache for his family, for the sons now distant memories mingling with the dust.

The parking lot was barely recognizable, a graveyard of vehicles, each one a silent sentinel to the day the world changed. But there, amidst the carnage, Dale's old green Dodge truck sat, an unexpected relic untouched by time's cruel hand. It wore a shroud of gray dust, a thin veil that Dale swept aside with the reverence of a man unearthing a treasure long thought lost. He fished in his pocket for the ignition key that had been untouched since it was placed in there before he began his last normal shift, a reminder of better times.

Dale blew the dust from the key hole, gave it a turn, and popped the door open with a harder-than-usual tug. "Here goes nothing," he muttered, as he slid the key into the ignition with hands that knew every inch of that truck, but this time with hope that she would be their savior. He turned it.

A moment of hesitation, a collective held breath—the pause between lightning and thunder—then the engine roared to life. The sound shattered the stillness, a defiant cry that seemed to rally the very air around them.

"Hot damn!!" Perry couldn't help but whoop, the Marine finding camaraderie in this victory over desolation as he stood outside the locked passenger door.

"Shhhhh," Dale motioned with his index finger to his masked lips as he reached over to give the door-lock knob a yank. "We don't know who, or what, is out there listening. They will surely pick up on the sound of our voices breaking the silence, if this old truck didn't already give us away," His mind was already turning, plotting routes, inventorying supplies.

"Right, sorry," Perry said, sheepish but undimmed as he plopped into the passenger seat. "So, we're mobile. What's next?"

"Next, we go back and start planning," Dale said, his gaze lingering on the horizon where the skeletal remains of trees reached for a sky that no longer promised dawn. "We've got a fighting chance now."

As he sat in the cab of the truck, surrounded by the ghosts of a life that once was, Dale allowed himself the luxury of a memory—a song on the radio, windows down, the Appalachian wind in his hair. And then, with the gravity of a man who knows the weight of the world rests upon his shoulders, he shifted the truck into Reverse and backed out of his usual spot for the last time.

As the truck lurched forward, Dale's fingers traced the rusted grooves of the truck's steering wheel between the cracks in the old blue and white UK Wildcats steering wheel cover, the engine's hum a welcome if not ominous companion in the silence. He shook his head at the memory of wanting to put a louder exhaust on her years ago since that is the last thing they needed given the current situation. As he squinted through the dusty windshield, a shadowy figure materialized from the ashen haze, its approach steady and purposeful.

"Someone's coming," Perry muttered, his hand reaching for the crowbar he'd noticed was wedged by his seat.

"Easy," Dale cautioned, his eyes never leaving the approaching silhouette. "We don't know friend or foe at this point in this new world."

The figure drew near, and the cloud of dust settled enough to reveal a woman with short red hair, her forehead smudged with grease and determination in her eyes. She walked with the sure-footedness of someone accustomed to navigating chaos, her nails rimmed with the dark evidence of hard work.

"Hey there," she called out, her voice muffled behind a heavy scarf that covered most of her nose and mouth "Wow, an actual running 5.9-liter V8! Sorry...I'm a mechanic, and damn if I haven't missed that sound over the last week and a half. Is she yours?"

"Depends on who's asking," Dale replied, his posture unyielding yet curious.

"I'm Flick. Or Felicity Williams in all my old yearbooks." She stopped a few feet away from the truck, eyeing the vehicle with unintentional professional interest. "Looks like you got lucky with the EMP. I haven't seen an engine so much as turn over, and believe me, I've tried a boat load."

"How have you been able to get around? I'm sure it's hard to breath in this dirty air if you're in it for long periods of time," Dale replied.

“Walking in this nasty air is rough, not to mention hazardous. Of course, I don’t know you two from Adam, but I haven’t seen another soul in this area,” Flick added, looking them over more closely. “The next town up may have people, but cell phones are fried and no one uses land lines anymore. Bicycle tires go flat in no time with all the debris scattered across the roadways, so I’ve been hoofing it in between flats, looking for any sign of civilization. I mean you guys no harm, and I hope the feeling is mutual."

"Well, believe it or not, we are the good guys," Dale acknowledged. He stepped out of the truck with a calculated and deliberate pace and shook her hand. "I’m Dale, and this here is Perry. We were working down in the mine when the closest blast hit us and knocked us out of commission for a bit. We have a small group, trying to find a way to survive. You seem to have done ok since it all happened. Tell us about your background, if you don’t mind my asking.”

"Well, I know a thing or two about survival, but this has definitely added a degree of difficulty," Flick said with a wry grin that didn't quite reach her eyes. "Tried my hand at Survivor a couple times, and some other reality shows. Studied every survival trick in the book and then some. I can build pretty much any kind of shelter and live off the land. I'd been sharing what I know on a podcast up until... well, you know."

"Sounds like you might be just who we need," Perry chimed in, sizing her up with an appraising glance.

"Is your group planning on holing up in those mines?" Flick gestured toward the clearly marked Mine #25 entrance with a jerk of her chin. "You'll need more than luck."

"That's the idea," Dale confirmed. His thoughts drifted momentarily to his sons, hoping they had found similar havens. "We could use someone with your skills. We have three others in our group: a gal and two other fellas back at the mine. They were banged up when the blast hit, so we have been out tryin' to find what supplies we can and let 'em heal up. It isn't the fanciest of accommodations, but we work well together and are tryin' to make the most of it."

"Every meaningful thing I had in this world is gone now, so lead the way, if you think the rest of your group will be OK with it. I'm an outsider, but I want to show I can earn my keep," Flick said, her boots crunching over the debris as she fell into step beside them.

"Pretty sure they will be glad to have a fresh set of eyes and hands to help us be able to stay where we are. Our intentions are to build our own bunker, of sorts," Perry added. "A coal mine isn't for everyone, so you may not be a fan, but it will be the safest place around here if we can get it fortified and proper air-flow and filtration. We've just put together a make-shift air filter, but we don't know how long it will last or how effective it will be. If you have any ideas or can improve what we've come up with, by all means feel free to chime in."

Together, they made a quick trip around the outer boundary of the mine property to make sure no one else was lurking about. Satisfied they were safe, they headed back in Dale's trusty old truck to the mine entrance. At Flick's suggestion, they attempted to hide the truck in plain sight, making it look as useless as possible in case anyone else stumbled upon the area like she did. She also suggested camouflaging the entrance to make it look as if the collapse sealed the fate of those inside and that it was not immediately noticeable from a distance. Perry took a pine tree limb and brushed it across the tire tracks and footprints in an effort to make the site look as desolate as everywhere else they had explored.

The trio entered the mine opening after they attempted to disguise the freshly drilled hole. TJ and Sam were kicked back resting in the quiet blackness on the mantrip and were both startled when Dale's headlamp danced across their faces. Almost in unison, both quickly sat up and fumbled for the knobs on their headlamps. "It's Dale! Sorry to startle you both. Meet Felic...er, Flick. Flick, meet TJ and Sam. We met her after we got my truck going. She has a plethora of knowledge of survival and how to build shelters, so she will add a lot of value to our group. And, she is a mechanic, which might help bring some of the equipment back to life. Rex will like some help getting what we need going again."

"I used to work on trucks like Dale's at the shop," Flick noted, her voice echoing off the walls. "Always liked the classics. And I've pretty much tinkered with everything that has gas or diesel running through it since I was a little girl. Bit of a Tom Boy, if you couldn't tell."

"Good to know. Hopefully you can keep her up and running in that nasty air. It's awful for us, and it can't be good for engines to breathe in, either. Glad mine can still fire up," Dale replied, filing away the information. Every skill, every bit of knowledge, was currency in this new world.

"Speaking of Rex, where is he?" asked Dale.

Sam replied, "Now, you know Rex. He wanted to stay at the work site and inventory everything we've found. Said he was going to use one of the air tanks to do that, since we were out of the danger zone staying up near the entrance. He wanted you and Perry to come see what he'd come up with so far when you got back."

The group loaded up the mantrip with their new member and slowly reached the depths of the mine, where the air grew cooler and the weight of the mountain pressed close. It was here that they began to use their expertise to forge a sanctuary from the bones of the earth.

As the group approached a partially collapsed support beam section, Flick asked Perry to stop the buggy and offered her insight on how to reinforce the once-sturdy supports. Once they reached their new home base, Flick got to work immediately in an effort to gain trust and earn her keep. She introduced herself to Rex, who took a quick liking to her energy and willingness to contribute to their survival efforts.

Flick's movements to reinforce the damaged support structures around the debris-covered equipment were efficient, while Dale orchestrated the placement of the heavier pieces of replacement materials, each piece a step toward sustainability. The rhythmic clank of metal against stone underscored their labor, a testament to their resolve.

"Never thought I'd be building a bunker," Perry said, wiping sweat from his brow as he secured a screen in place with duct tape.

"None of us did," Dale responded, his voice steady as the beat of a hammer. "But we adapt. We survive."

"Like those old country songs I used to hear you belting out from your truck, huh?" Perry teased, though his smile faltered in the dim light.

"Something like that," Dale agreed quietly, allowing himself only a moment of nostalgia before refocusing on the task at hand.

Hours passed, marked by the steady progress of their hands and the slow bonding of shared purpose. In the shelter of the Appalachian mines, amidst the ruin of the world above, they carved out hope, one filter, one beam, one solid wall at a time.

Dale, with his fingers coated in the constant dust of the mine, carefully traced the edges of the makeshift filter while Flick skillfully handled the tape. The sound of tearing mesh blended with their quiet breaths in the expansive space. The muted light from their headlamps cast long shadows over the framework they had assembled.

"Make sure it's tight," Flick instructed, her voice echoing slightly off the walls. "Any gap could let in more than just air."

He nodded, pressing firmly where she directed. The filters, scavenged from the guts of old machinery, were a patchwork of necessity. Flick had repurposed them with an ingenuity born of desperation, fashioning a system that might just keep them breathing untainted air.

"Fan's in place," Perry announced, stepping back from the contraption they'd rigged to circulate fresh air into their underground haven. It was a Frankenstein's monster of equipment: spare parts brought to life for a singular purpose. Dale eyed the setup, the weight of its importance settling heavy on his chest.

"Nice work," Dale managed, though his throat felt like it was coated in soot. The slow churn of the fan blades began, an unsteady waltz against the silence that once dominated the mine.

"Let's hope it holds," Flick said, catching Dale's eye with a look that spoke volumes of shared uncertainties. Her freckles stood out against her pale skin, a stark reminder of the sun they all missed.

A pause stretched between them, filled only by the mechanical hum and the distant drip of water. Then, almost reluctantly, Dale broke it with a question that had been gnawing at him. "Tell me about your family, Flick."

She wiped her hands on her jeans, a smear of grease marking the denim. "My brother," she started, her voice suddenly soft, "he taught me everything I know about engines. We'd spend hours in the garage, just... tinkering."

"Think he made it?" Perry asked, gingerly taking a seat on a chunk of fallen rock.

"God, I hope so, but I doubt many did," Flick whispered, her gaze distant.

Dale listened, the stories weaving through the stale air, each tale a thread in the tapestry of what had been. He thought of his own kin, scattered like leaves in a wind too fierce to fight. His heart clenched at the memory of laughter and bickering, now as distant as the clear blue sky.

"Kinda feels like a family," Flick lamented, a smile tugging at the corner of her mouth despite the gravity of their situation. "A bunch of miners and a mechanic. Who would've thought?"

"Appalachia breeds tough folk," Perry added with a shrug. "We'll make do."

The conversation lulled, each lost in their thoughts as the fan continued its laborious spin. The bunker around them, crude and improvised, stood as a monument to their resolve. In the face of annihilation, they had found a semblance of home, a shelter not just from the fallout but from the solitude that threatened to consume them.

"Alright," Dale said eventually, standing up. "Let's check the seals one more time. Can't be too careful."

With a collective nod, they returned to their work, the task grounding them. They moved together, a unit bound by more than just survival — bound by the unspoken vow to hold onto their humanity, no matter how dark the world outside became.

Dale slumped against the cool stone wall of the bunker, his chest rising and falling with measured breaths. The others were scattered around him, their forms slack with exhaustion amidst the makeshift beds and salvaged furniture. The air was thick with the scent of earth and metal, a constant reminder of their subterranean existence. A dim helmet light flickered overhead, casting long shadows that danced along the jagged walls.

There was a pause in their labor, a rare moment of stillness in the relentless struggle for survival. Dale's eyes traced the lines of the bunker, the rough-hewn refuge they had cobbled together from the bowels of the mountains that had once provided their livelihood. He could hear the distant whir of the jury-rigged air filtration system, a rhythm that pulsed like a heartbeat through the space.

"Never thought I'd be grateful for all those years underground," he murmured, almost to himself.

"Feels almost normal, doesn't it?" Perry chuckled weakly from across the room. His face was smeared with grime, the blueish light casting deep hollows under his eyes.

"Normal." Dale snorted softly. "If you can call this normal."

The group fell silent again, each lost in the weight of their reality. Yet, beneath the fatigue, there flickered something else—a glimmer of hope. They had done the impossible, turned their prison into protection. It was a testament to their resilience, to the strength that had been honed in the depths of the Appalachian mines.

"Can't stay holed up here forever, though," Flick said after a time, breaking the silence as she inspected her dirt-stained nails. "We're going to need more supplies if we're gonna last. Food, water... maybe even some parts for the truck. I'm gonna need to modify the air intake to keep out the particles. That will kill any good air-breathing engine."

"Right," Dale agreed, pushing himself off the wall with a groan. His muscles protested, but he ignored them. "Soon as we've caught our breath, we head out. There's gotta be something left in those towns, something we can use."

"Could be dangerous," Perry warned, his voice low. "Not just the fallout, but who knows what else is out there now. Desperation does ugly things to folks, and other survivors we run across might not be as personable as Flick."

"Which is why we go prepared," Dale responded, the firmness in his tone brooking no argument. "We stick together, watch each other's backs. We're miners, remember? We've faced cave-ins, gas leaks... We can handle a few scavengers."

"Or whatever else might be waiting for us out there," Flick added, a steely edge to her words.

"Then it's settled." Dale straightened, looking at his makeshift family—one forged not by blood but by circumstance. "We rest tonight. Tomorrow, we start planning. We map out the nearby towns, figure out the safest routes, take inventory of what we got and what we need. We're survivors. We'll find a way to keep surviving."

"Survivors," Perry echoed, nodding slowly.

"Appalachian survivors," Flick corrected with a hint of pride, despite the gloom that hung over them like a shroud.

As the conversation waned, Dale felt the weight of leadership settle onto his shoulders, a familiar burden from days long gone. But this time, it wasn't about coal—it was about life itself. With a final glance around the bunker, he let his gaze linger on each member of the crew. They were weary, yes, but not broken. Not yet.

"Get some sleep," he instructed gently. "Tomorrow, we face the world again."

In the quiet that followed, Dale allowed himself a small smile. Their progress was a beacon in the darkness, a signal that even now, humanity could find ways to endure.

Dale watched as Flick used a shard of glass to dissect a mushroom, her red hair catching the dim light filtering through their makeshift air filter. Her steady hands belied the urgency of their lesson.

"See here?" she pointed to the gills underneath its cap. "These are fine and even—safe enough. But you eat the wrong kind, and it's a one-way ticket out of this life."

The crew, rugged faces pinched with concentration, leaned in around the small circle of light. They were miners, not foragers, but the rules had changed. Their survival depended on adapting, on learning skills that lay outside the comfort of coal seams and heavy machinery.

"Same goes for water," Flick continued, motioning towards a collection of plastic bottles rigged with charcoal and sand. "You can't trust a clear stream just because it looks pure. We purify everything."

"Seems like a lot of trouble for a sip of water. We found an underground stream years ago about midway through the mine. Tests they did on it made it seem fine," Perry muttered, his voice echoing slightly off the stone walls of the bunker.

"Trouble is a small price for staying alive. We need to make sure we can filter that stream water as thoroughly as possible, but we need to find where it starts. Radiation can't be filtered from water, unfortunately, so unless it starts deep down in this mountain, away from the fallout, it's too risky to use," Dale interjected, his tone solemn, eyes scanning the attentive group. "Might not be able to find much bottled water anywhere near here that survived the nukes, so we need to make that a priority. What we have won't last but a few more days."

He felt the weight of each gaze upon him—their anchor in a world adrift. He nodded at Flick to proceed while he contemplated their next steps, the critical preparations that could mean the difference between life and death. "Let's move on to gear," Dale announced. "We need to be ready for anything out there."

They moved as one, gathering near the stash of supplies they'd amassed thus far. Canned goods, medical kits, lengths of rope—all remnants of a world now foreign. Dale picked up a hunting knife, its blade glinting dully. Weapons had become necessary allies, and he distributed them with a reverence born of necessity.

"Keep these on you at all times," he instructed, his voice gruff with emotion. "They're not just tools; they're lifelines."

The others took their weapons, handling them with care that spoke of the gravity they all felt. There was no bravado here, only the quiet understanding that survival hinged on being prepared.

"Check your packs," Dale said, moving on to a stack of worn backpacks. "Food, water, first-aid. Don't overload; we move faster light."

"Fast and light," Perry echoed, stuffing his pack with jerky and bottled water.

"Remember, stick together," Dale added, his words painting the image of unity that had always been the core of any mining team he'd led. "Out there, it's not just about the individual. We're a family. We watch out for each other."

Flick nodded, securing her own pack, her expression somber yet determined. They were an unlikely family, bound by circumstance and a shared goal—to endure.

As the last straps were tightened and the final checks made, Dale allowed himself a slow survey of the faces around him. These were the faces of Appalachian resilience, chiseled by both nature and hardship. They were ready, or as ready as they could be, for the world beyond the mine's protective embrace.

"Alright," he said, his voice resonating with the authority that had carried him through countless shifts under the earth. "Let's get some rest. Come sunrise, we reclaim what's ours."

And as the shadows grew long within the bunker, Dale felt the familiar twinge of anticipation mixed with dread. They were stepping into the unknown, but they would face it as they had faced the dark tunnels below the mountains—with resolve and the unwavering hope of finding light on the other side.

Dale scooped the last spoonful of beans from his tin plate, the metallic scrape echoing faintly against the stone walls of the bunker. He watched as Perry passed a dented flask of water to Flick, who accepted it with a nod, her grease-stained hands a testament to the work they'd done. The flicker of makeshift candles cast shadows upon their solemn faces, each one etched with lines of worry and wear.

"Never thought I'd miss the mess hall," Dale murmured, the corners of his mouth twitching into the ghost of a smile, "or gas station coffee."

"Or my mom's overcooked roast," Perry added, earning a low chuckle from the group.

The laughter was short-lived, dissipating into the cool air like vapor. They were miners, used to the bowels of the earth, but this—this was different. This was survival stripped down to its marrow.

"Y'all," Dale began, voice steady as bedrock, "we been through storms before. Seen collapses, faced off with blackdamp and fire. But we always came out on top because we had each other's backs."

Heads nodded in the dim light, eyes locking onto his.

"Out there," he continued, gesturing toward the makeshift hatch that stood between them and the ravaged world beyond, "ain't no different. We stick together. We survive. For the memories of our families. For us."

Flick leaned forward, her presence as formidable as any of the men. "We got skills most don't," she said, her voice firm. "And I ain't just talking about turning wrenches. We can make it out there."

Their meal finished, the clatter of utensils settling like the finality of a judge's gavel, the crew rose to their feet. Each movement was deliberate, the weight of their impending journey grounding them to the earth they'd once excavated.

With the last bites of their dinner cleared, Dale led the way to the bunker's entrance. A heavy dust-covered tarp served as their final barrier. His hand hovered over the rough fabric, every fiber of his being coiled tight as underground cables. He turned to face his comrades and saw a familiar resolve looking back at him.

"Alright," he said, his voice the only sound in the cavernous space. "Let's see what tomorrow holds for us."

After a restless night, one by one, they shouldered their packs, the contents a catalog of survival: cans of food, bottles of murky water, tools of their former trade repurposed for this new life. Backs straightened under the burden, not just of the gear, but of the hope they carried—that somewhere out there, they could carve out a piece of the world still worth living in.

Dale lifted the tarp, revealing the first slivers of dawn's light filtering through the debris. The air was heavy with the scent of ash and the unknown, but beneath it was something else—a faint whisper of pine and soil, a reminder of the Appalachian wilderness that had endured long before them. "Mask up before we get going. That's the one thing we can do to help ourselves endure this filthy air."

"Stay sharp," he instructed, his gaze sweeping over the group. "Remember your training, mind your surroundings, and keep an eye on each other."

As they stepped through the threshold, the world greeted them with silence, a vast emptiness that held both threat and promise. Dale felt the familiar surge of adrenaline, the same rush that came with descending into the depths of a new vein of coal. Except this time, they weren't delving into darkness; they were emerging from it, seeking the light of a future only they could forge.

"Let's move out," Dale commanded, as the cadence of survivors marching towards the uncertainty of the new world order echoed among them.

As the darkness settled upon the mine property, the headlights of Dale's Dodge crept towards the entrance with the day's pluckings from the closest towns. Dale had driven Sam and TJ to their former homes, only to discover there was nothing to go back to. Each of them lived alone, as did Dale, whose home was unrecognizable. Despite their large haul of items to help fill various needs, the trio of survivors silently dealt with their own struggles on the somber return trip. Entire mountain towns had been wiped away as if they were sandcastles in the way of an ocean tide. Dale was unsure how widespread the devastation reached, but he knew that it would be a miracle if anyone from his group had family and friends who survived.

As Dale dropped the tailgate, Rex and Flick walked out to meet them and help unload the truck bed. Rex looked upon Dale's face and remarked, "That bad, huh?"

Dale nodded his head, fighting the urge to look away from Rex. "We checked the areas where our homes... used to be. Checked yours, too, buddy," Dale barely uttered aloud. "Bastards took everything from us. And everyone around us. Who knows about further out, like where my boys are, up near Lexington," Dale squeezed out as his eyes welled up, teeth gritted together. "Hope to God we can figure out a way to check on those loved ones once we can get settled in here. Get our sanctuary built up."

Rex looked at the ground, then back at Dale, "We will, D. Gotta create somethin' worth fighting for here, in case there's nothin' left anywhere else." The dust from their protective coats fluttered as the two men hugged each other for reassurance.

Chapter 7
Playing Defense

During their most recent excursion into the outskirts of the nearest town, the group was able to find many useful items. They searched through standing and collapsed dwellings, finding several personal protection handguns, two rifles, and a shotgun. They also collected a decent haul of ammunition and other much-needed supplies. However, the discovery of former occupants in various stages of decomposition was unnerving, but the group realized the gravity of the situation. They saw numerous indications of activity among different sections of ruins, including grocery stores and hardware shops. The group understood that their bunker's discovery was not a matter of if, but when. Therefore, they needed to formulate a plan to protect what they had.

Dale worked with a methodical precision as he assigned the newly acquired weapons among his trusted crew. He surveyed the sanctuary around them and felt a warmth from the resilience nestled within the once vibrant heart of coal country.

"Sam, you'll be our eyes. Stay sharp, and once we locate something a little more powerful, it's yours. For now, this will do," Dale instructed, handing her the .22 rifle. With a ponytail reminiscent of her high school years, Sam's youthful face revealed a focused gaze honed on the shooting range, where she had spent a great deal of time as a rifle team gold medalist.

"Rex, I need your knowledge of this place. Set up traps where you can." The older man, his gray hair a contrast to his still nimble fingers, gave a curt nod, understanding the labyrinth of tunnels could be as much a weapon as any firearm.

Perry stood close, his military stance seemingly out of place with the rugged miners around him. "We secure every path to the entrance. Barricades here, here, and here," Dale said, pointing to the rough map they had sketched out on an old piece of cardboard. Perry's jaw set firm, it echoed the presence of the recently acquired AR-15 that was slung across his back, both ready for any confrontation, his usually hot-headed nature now an asset in the planning of their defense.

The group spread out, scavenging what they could from the mine's depths to fortify their stronghold. Wooden planks, broken tools, and scraps of metal were repurposed with urgency, transforming the abandoned shafts into a bastion against the chaos outside.

Over the course of the next two days, the group had been able to fortify a great deal, both inside and out. The first signs of trouble pierced the fragile silence of the second evening of those days while several members of the group were tweaking things outside. Footsteps, a hint of impending violence, echoed through the trees, and hushed voices crept toward the mine's mouth like poison seeping through cracks.

Dale's piercing whistle sent everyone into action, serving as an effective intrusion alert despite the lack of a formal system. Perry checked his AR-15, ensuring it was ready to spit fire if need be. Sam, ever the sharpshooter, quickly ascended the mountainside to duck behind a stack of carefully placed rocks on higher ground, her eyes narrowing as she peered down the rifle's sights.

The murmur of the approaching scavengers grew louder, their words indistinct but their intent clear as the last rays of daylight cast long shadows across the battered landscape. Dale felt the weight of the shotgun in his grip, the cool steel a welcome comfort at the moment and more useful up close than the Colt tucked into his waistband.

During their initial canvas of the mine property, one of the group members stumbled upon an old megaphone in an office building storage room. Although they didn't know why at the time, the member decided to grab it, thinking it might come in handy later on. Today, the megaphone would get some use of its intended purpose as Dale keyed the "TALK" button and announced, "To those who approach this mine: It is ours, and we will fiercely defend it. Turn back while you still can."

The rustling in the distance came to a halt. Hushed voices began a back and forth rapport from different areas of the surrounding woods and landscape. “Good to know, but you are wrong. It’s our mine now,” sounded a booming voice that no doubt was the leader of the gang. With that declaration, several pitches of “Wooo!!” and “Hell yeah!!!” sounded out, and the rustling started again at a much more intense pace.

"Well, gang, I tried. Just remember what we're fighting for," he growled, as he chucked the now-useless megaphone into a pile of scrap. It was for family, for survival, for a sliver of hope in a world that seemed determined to extinguish it—the latter, in the form of an unrelenting gang of scavengers.

TJ spoke up with an unusually serious tone, “Saw somethin’ once that said: If you have no choice but to fight, then fight like you’re the third monkey on the ramp to Noah’s Ark—”.

From above them, Sam chimed in, “And brother, it’s starting to rain.”

Dale grinned. “I like it. Sounds like we just found our battle cry.”

The tension coiled within the sanctuary was as palpable as the mountain mists that clung to the trees. Every breath held the promise of conflict, every heartbeat a drumbeat to battle. And as the sun dipped below the horizon, staining the sky with blood-red hues, Dale Rogers and his crew braced for the storm that was rushing toward them.

As the scavenger gang approached with loud, heavy steps, their dark figures gathered into a threatening formation near the mine's entrance. Dale Rogers stood confidently, holding his shotgun at the ready amidst the chaos.

"Stand strong!" Dale's words echoed and filled them with courage, reminding them of their own resilience in the face of adversity. The crew stood taller, ready to face whatever challenges the intruders presented.

TJ, stationed at a critical juncture near the main entrance, squared his shoulders, his lean frame deceptive in its ability to withstand the impending onslaught. He gripped a repurposed rusty pick-axe, ready to engage anyone within its reach.

The defenders stood firm, their resolve unwavering as they repelled the relentless onslaught. Each clash only fueled their determination to protect what was theirs at all costs. The territory at their backs was all they had.

The coolness of the boulder pressed against Sam Thompson's back as she hunkered down behind a tactically erected barricade of sandbags and rusted iron sheets. Her breaths came in controlled bursts, the only sound louder than her heartbeat was the sporadic crack of her rifle. She peered through the scope, eyes scanning for the silhouette of invaders in the distance. The setting sun cast long shadows across the battlefield, creating an eerie contrast against the flashes of gunfire. Sam's training kicked in, her focus unwavering as she remained vigilant for any movement in the darkness ahead.

"Steady, Sam," Dale whispered from a few feet away, a nod towards the young coal-miner who had only mentioned her high school sharpshooter competitions in passing during night shifts. Now, those skills were a lifeline. Sam's determination was visibly etched into the tightness of her jaw. A flicker of movement caught her eye, and without hesitation, she took another shot, the bullet finding its mark with crippling precision.

"Hit another one," she muttered, her voice devoid of triumph. This was about survival, not sport.

TJ whirled towards the sounds of moving gravel and swung the pick-axe with a swift follow-up strike, he incapacitated the enemy, his heart pounding with the adrenaline of battle as he scanned the dark cavern for any more threats.

"Keep 'em back!" Dale commanded, the pump shotgun's report a punctuation mark to his orders. He was a dedicated guardian, his life in these mountains having taught him the unforgiving law of nature—adapt or perish. Each round he fired was a testament to his resolve, the buckshot a defender of the sanctuary they had carved from the remnants of a shattered world.

The attackers continued to press forward, their numbers overwhelming, but TJ refused to back down, determined to protect his makeshift family at all costs. With each strike and dodge, he silently vowed to never let them down, no matter the odds stacked against them.

The battle raged on, the evening air heavy with the scent and sounds of combat. Dale moved through the fray, his actions deliberate, each crack of the shotgun measured and precise. The scent of gunpowder mingled with the metallic hint of blood, a visceral reminder of the stakes at hand.

"Push them out!" Dale's voice, raw from shouting, cut through the turmoil. It carried the weight of a leader's responsibility, the burden of a father's protection, and the unyielding spirit of a generation that refused to be extinguished.

As the scavengers faltered under their relentless defense, Dale charged forward and cracked off the last rounds of his shotgun towards the last wave of three aggressors, leading the charge against the invaders with a ferocity that surprised even himself. The stakes were high, but he knew failure was not an option. He wanted to set the tone for this group and any others that might try to take the only home they have. Two of the semi-hard-chargers caught several of the double-ought buck in the thigh and calf areas and quickly turned-tail. Dale was not looking for kill shots, only to send a resounding message.

“You ain’t takin’ this damn mine,” Dale said as a reinforcement of the actions exhibited by his new family. The remaining scavengers began to retreat into the gloom from which they came, most helping.

Perry moved like a shadow at Dale's side, his training manifesting in short, controlled bursts. He communicated with hand signals, guiding their comrades without wasting precious breath. They were outmanned, but the crew's coordination held the line, each miner a wall of defense against the onslaught.

"Push 'em back!" Perry yelled, the strain in his voice betraying the ferocity of their situation.

The battle raged in harsh grunts and the clatter of metal. The sanctuary, once a haven of solidarity, now shook with the violence of invasion. Dust rose like mist, and the acrid smell of blood mingled with the earthiness of the underground. It was a dance of survival, every step a fight to preserve what little they had left in a world gone mad.

"Stand firm!" Dale cried out, his voice cutting through the din. Here in the depths of Appalachia, they would make their stand, their unity their shield against the encroaching darkness. They were miners, sons, daughters, protectors—and they would not yield.

Dale's knuckles whitened around the grip of an iron wrench. The scavengers surged forward, a tide of desperation and lawlessness that sought to sweep away the fragile peace of their sanctuary. "Come on, you bastards," Dale muttered under his breath.

A figure lunged at him waving a piece of jagged rebar. With a grunt, Dale sidestepped, swinging the wrench with precision from countless hours chipping away at stubborn coal seams. Metal met bone with a sickening crunch, and the scavenger crumpled. The adrenaline coursing through his veins dulled the sensation of what he had just done, but Dale knew that in this unforgiving world, it was kill or be killed. He wiped the blood from his wrench on the fallen enemy's coat and continued on his journey, determined to survive no matter the cost.

Another assailant took his place, this one more deceptive, waiting for an opening. But Dale was a true miner whose patience and perseverance were his creed. He stepped back slightly to draw the attacker in, then delivered a swift kick to the knee, followed by a downward blow that sent the man sprawling into the dirt. The wrench again found its target. Dale kept his head on a continuous swivel, immediately resetting his stance, like pulling an arrow into a bow.

The success of their mission depended on their ability to maintain control in the midst of the storm. Perry, a few paces away, nodded, showing his experience as a seasoned soldier. Together, they moved in perfect sync, like a well-coordinated team who knew the significance of protecting their stronghold.

The scavengers' initial ferocity waned, their numbers dwindling under the relentless defense mounted by Dale and his people. Through sheer grit and dogged determination, they turned the tide, step by painstaking step. A pickaxe found its mark, a shovel acting as a shield, mining equipment pieces repurposed into instruments of survival. Each tool told a story, not of extraction, but of protection—of the lifeblood of a community that refused to be extinguished.

"Fall back!" came the ragged cry from the invaders, defeat evident in their collective tone. The sanctuary had held, a diamond in its disheveled surroundings and barren landscape.

Dale stood wearily, the fight faded from his arms and legs as he watched the scavengers retreat into the shadows from whence they came. His heart pounded like a drum, resonating deep within him. Around him, his crew caught their breath, their gazes meeting his in silent accord. They were not just survivors; they were protectors of their remaining home.

Dale's chest heaved as he let out a breath he didn't realize he had been holding, feeling a sense of relief wash over him. He scanned the dimly lit areas around their sanctuary, the mine that had become both home and fortress. His crew was a patchwork family forged in adversity, each one pausing as if to ensure the danger had truly passed.

"Check on everyone," Dale instructed. "Make sure we're all still in one piece."

"Sam, you hit?" TJ called out.

"Nah, just grazed," Sam replied, her tone steady despite the blood trickling down her arm. "I've had worse playin' in the woods."

"Rex, traps still set?" Dale continued, his eyes lingering on the entryway where the last of the scavengers had disappeared.

"Mostly intact," Rex confirmed, wiping sweat from his brow. "But we'll need to reset them before nightfall."

"Good work." Dale's nod indicative of his pride in his crew.

He moved with purpose around the rough exterior of the mine entrance. The makeshift barricades bore the marks of the attack, splintered wood and twisted metal testimony to the scavengers' desperation. Dale knew any worse of an attack would truly push the limits of his crew and their make-shift fortress. They had been successful with their first test, but Dale had a feeling this was the first of many to come once word got around of their stronghold.

"Structural damage?" he asked Perry, who was already surveying the integrity of their defenses.

"Nothing critical, but we can't let our guard down," Perry responded, his military-trained eyes missing nothing.

"Let's shore up these weak points," Dale ordered, pointing to a section of wall that had taken a beating. "We'll reinforce it with whatever we can scavenge from the lower levels."

"Everyone, take five, then we're back at it," Dale declared, though his own rest would wait. "We need to remove the dead to the outskirts from which they came. They can come back for 'em, or it can send a message to any others with the same intent." There was much to be done, and daylight was a precious commodity they couldn't afford to waste.

"Copy that," TJ grunted, leaning heavily against a support beam, his knuckles raw from the fight.

"Five minutes," Dale echoed to himself, feeling the ache in his own bones. The silence in the wake of battle lay heavy upon them, a shroud of uncertainty about what tomorrow might bring. But this rare moment of downtime was earned—a chance to tend to wounds, to steel their resolve, and to remember why they fought so fiercely.

For now, the enemy had been driven back into the chaos of the world above, but Dale knew the respite was temporary. They would come again, hungrier and more numerous. And when they did, the guardians of the sanctuary would stand ready—undaunted, unbowed, unbroken.

After a few minutes had passed, Dale's gaze swept over his weary crew, their faces smeared with the residue of battle and determination. They stood in a ragged circle, catching their breaths, . The mine's confines echoed with the distant drip of water—a reminder that nature cared little for human squabbles.

"Listen up," Dale's voice cut through the stillness, commanding attention. His words were deliberate, each a testament to their survival. "This fight ain't the last. It's just a taste of what's out there, waiting to claw its way in."

He walked among them, the beam from his headlamp casting stark shadows on the tunnel walls. He stopped by Sam, nodding approvingly as she checked her rifle with while a nearly-dried stream of blood traced the outline of her arm. TJ leaned against a wall, catching Dale's eye with a nod that spoke of unspoken respect forged in the heat of combat.

"Y'all did good today—real good. But we can't let our guard down. Not for one second." Dale's eyes hardened to emphasize his point to the crew. "We're all that's left of this world. Our families, our homes...the memories of all of 'em—they're counting on us to carry on in their places."

Perry, standing tall despite the fatigue etched into his features, met Dale's gaze. A silent understanding passed between them—the weight of leadership, the burden of decisions that could mean life or death.

"Let's take what we learned today and build on it. Fortify every choke point to the entrance, double-check every barricade. Rex," Dale said, turning to address the keeper of traps, "You rig this place tight enough to make a rat think twice about squeezing through. They didn't make it inside, thank God, but when word gets out we have a resilient group and a decent hideaway, they'll come in droves trying to take what we've got."

Nods of agreement continued through the group. Their resolve, a collective will to endure no matter the cost.

"Unity is our strength," Dale continued, his voice a low rumble in the cavernous space. "Together, we've got a fighting chance. We aren't a big group by any standards, but by God, we are a mean bunch of sumbitches who have each other's backs."

He paused, letting the gravity of his words sink in. Every face reflected back at him was a mirror of his own resolve—hardened by loss, yet not without hope.

"Rest up now. Tomorrow, we start again." Dale's declaration hung in the air, a solemn vow to the future they all fought to secure.

As his crew dispersed to their appointed tasks, Dale remained steadfast, a solitary figure against the backdrop of uncertainty. The Appalachian mountains above may have crumbled under the weight of the apocalypse, but below, in the heart of the earth, his spirit stood unbroken.

Chapter 8
Gathering Necessities

Weeks had passed since the world had changed, and with every abandoned homestead they encountered, the reality of their situation grew heavier. Unburied bodies lay where they had fallen, their untended graves a grim testimony to the suddenness of the catastrophe. The group tried to cover each one they came to with whatever they could find nearby. It was the least they could do to pay forward what little human decency still existed in the current times.

The excursions to gather what supplies they could find, whether it was a general sweep or to find something in particular, were consistently alarming at first with each body they came across. However, the regularity of the discoveries of the deceased had begun to cause a calloused shell to form around each group member's psyche.

Dale strategically parked his truck behind the remnants of two rickety buildings. Sam volunteered to stay with the truck in case someone saw it passing by. As the small group trudged forward, he scanned the horizon where skeletal trees seemed propped up against the dreary gray backdrop of both mountains and sky. Every so often, Dale would pause, listening for any sound that didn't belong to the wind or the rustling of leaves. But there was only silence—a testament to the changed world.

"Keep your eyes peeled," Dale muttered. TJ, the younger miner with nerves like live wires, nodded and shifted his gaze back and forth across the desolate landscape. Perry kept his hand near the pistol they'd found earlier, the weight of his Marine Corps training visible in his always-ready stance. "Nothing but ghosts," Perry muttered, his gaze lingering on an empty children's playground that swayed eerily in the wind.

"Let's move on," Dale said. "There's a place TJ knows, might still have supplies." They trudged forward, the shrouded sun a quiet observer in the gray sky. Every so often, Dale would pause, listening for any sound that didn't belong to the wind or the rustling of leaves. But there was only silence—a testament to the changed world.

As they approached the outskirts of what used to be a bustling town, the barely-tethered sign of a store came into view. "Over there," TJ pointed towards the outcrop of half-collapsed buildings. "That's Miller's Sporting Goods. If anything's left, we'll find it there."

"Looks like someone's been there, but maybe they didn't get everything," TJ said, hope in his voice. "This building has seen better days—might be what spooked 'em."

Dale led the way with a steady and deliberate pace. The broken front window of the store stood out like a wound on the building's face. He paused, listening for any sign of movement within. Satisfied, he signaled to his companions, and they slipped inside. "Let's find out," Dale responded, leading the way with cautious steps.

A thin layer of dust covered the floor, undisturbed except for a single set of footprints that led away from the broken window. The smell of mold and metal greeted them, mingling with the faint odor of decay. A quick sweep of their flashlights surprisingly revealed only a few rows of empty shelves, but it was what lay beyond that caught their attention.

"Jackpot," Perry whispered as the beam of his light settled on the firearms wall. Though several guns were missing, enough remained to bolster their arsenal—hunting rifles, shotguns, and boxes of ammunition. Since this was a small-town store, a large inventory of weapons wasn't expected, but what they found was more than enough to help their group.

"Looks like someone beat us here, but didn't have the means to carry much," Dale observed, his fingers brushing against the cool barrel of a rifle. "Luck shined down on us today."

"Never thought I'd be this grateful for football season," TJ joked dryly, trying to lighten the mood.

"Let's just hope we won't have to use this stuff," Dale replied, though he knew the likelihood of confrontation was high. "Come on, let's keep moving."

The group worked efficiently, nearly filling up Dale's truck bed with clothing, coats, and shoes. Baseball bats, catcher's masks, helmets from various sports, and other protective sports gear were added to their haul—unconventional armor against an unpredictable world.

They gathered armloads of clothing—sturdy boots, jackets thick enough to ward off the winter chill, and layers that smelled faintly of mothballs but were whole and clean.

As they loaded the last of the supplies, Dale took one last look around the empty store. This wasn't just scavenging; it was salvaging pieces of a life they once knew. "Let's head back and try to find the local pharmacy on the way. It'd be great to find some meds and supplies to fight off infection and sickness before it all gets gathered up by other groups."

Dale's old Dodge crept down the debris-cluttered mountain roads, his eyes scanning for landmarks through the wasteland. A faded sign for Benson's Pharmacy appeared, its windows shattered from the blast but the structure largely intact—a good sign that looters might have overlooked it.

"Sam, TJ, you're with me," Dale directed as he pulled the truck behind the building. "Perry, keep watch. We need to be quick."

The air was thick with dust as they entered the pharmacy, the once sterile aisles now a disarray of spilled medicine and broken glass. Sam headed straight for the feminine hygiene and antiseptic aisles, while TJ's flashlight scanned over the labels of antibiotics and pain relievers.

"Found some amoxicillin, ciprofloxacin, and a bunch of acetaminophen," TJ announced.

"Good. Grab all you can carry," Dale replied, stuffing cold remedies into his backpack. The first aid supplies were next—bandages, antiseptics, gauze—all essentials for their makeshift infirmary back at camp.

They worked quickly and efficiently, knowing every minute inside was a risk. As they loaded the last of their finds into Dale's truck, Perry signaled from the lookout point.

"Got company," he mouthed, nodding toward an approaching figure.

"Inside, now!" Dale quietly ordered, ushering his group back into the pharmacy. They watched as the figure, another survivor by the looks of it, passed by without noticing them.

"Close call," TJ whispered once the coast was clear.

"Let's not push our luck. Time to get out of here," Dale said. As they drove away, the store disappearing behind them, Dale allowed himself a moment of quiet reflection. The simple act of scavenging had become a lifeline, a way to claw back from the edge of despair.

As the group returned to the mine, they lamented on the turn of the times from as normal as they could know to having to scrap and fight for their very survival in a matter of weeks. Food supplies were running short in their storage area, and the places they'd driven to had been mostly gone through. From time to time, they would run upon an isolated cash-and-carry or small variety store that hadn't been discovered, but those were getting to be few and far between.

Rex and Flick helped unload the day's capture and quickly took the supplies inside to inventory and prepare for distribution or storage. The amount of items were much more than they'd expected to pick up, but they knew they had to strike while the iron was hot to have a chance at still finding the items Dale, TJ, Perry, and Sam had brought in this truck load.

Dale addressed the group as each member made repeat trips between their new home and his Dodge. "The next order of business will be to find fuel. This truck was almost full when she was dragged into action, but our recon and scavenger trips have made the old girl thirsty again. Without electricity, underground fuel tanks at most modern stations were built to thwart the efforts of thieves, but a hand crank pump could still access certain styles for smaller amounts.

Flick had located a hand crank pump at a hardware store among the few items that had been looked over by looters and scavengers. With her background of working on motor vehicles, she knew something like that would prove useful once the fuel in Dale's truck ran out. Although he'd topped off just before disaster struck, and they hadn't been venturing out very far on their excursions, it would only last so long.

The following morning, Dale, Flick, and TJ went to the fuel station they'd passed on their way back from the previous evening's venture, in hopes no one had attempted to extract the gasoline and damaged the access port that's normally locked on the ground. If the port was undamaged, the hand crank pump could extract fuel by following some tried and true procedures to bypass the locks and safety measures. Flick claimed to know someone who has been able to do this successfully and that she was taught by the best during her wilder days of her youth. The older underground tank setups lack the backup safety measures found in the new ones.

They arrived at the abandoned old gas station where Flick demonstrated her resourcefulness once more. Using a crow-bar, she was able to quickly and carefully gain access below the ground locks. With the hand-crank pump and a long thin hose, she began extracting gasoline from the underground tanks. Dale had rounded up half a dozen empty gas cans, each with a capacity of five gallons.

"Might want to hurry this operation up, since the early-risers might just want to get in on our little party," TJ suggested while keeping his head on a swivel.

"How 'bout them apples?" Flick asked Dale, who could only grin and shake his head at her skillset. She had fuel pulsing through the lengthy clear line in seemingly no time, resulting in a beaming smile across Flick's face.

TJ guided the fresh fuel into the cans one by one, and within 15 minutes they had enough to fill up the old Dodge's nearly barren 25-gallon tank. Dale poured each filled container into the thirsty tank as soon as it was relayed to him.

Once it was topped off, the cans were filled again to capacity by Flick's meticulous work. "Barely spilled a drop! Should keep the curious folks from thinking twice about pullin' off what I just did. Hell, looks like we were never here!"

"Nice job, Flick. Couldn't have pulled this off without ya," Dale said with pride and with further affirmation they'd made a great addition to their group. "This'll definitely help us be able to reach further outside the areas we've searched so far—for more supplies and maybe even more solid help for our group, like you've been."

Flick's cheeks flushed red with embarrassment that she tried to hide by turning her head as she finished cleaning around the tank access. "Thanks, Dale. I'm so glad I've been able to contribute. I haven't been with you folks all that long, but you feel as much like my family as any I've had in a long time."

"Yeah, we sure are glad you came along, Flick. Hopefully we can find more good folk like you to add to our numbers. Speakin' of which, I've wondered if any of the other local mines have had similar situations like we have. Other night shifts were finishing up, just like we were..." TJ remarked with a concerned tone.

“Damn, don't know why I hadn’t thought of that, TJ. I bet you’re right, and they might not have had the same end result,” Dale replied in a pondering tone. “Closest one is about ten minutes away—Mine #29. We did a Mine Rescue training there about 15 years ago, so I have an idea of the layout...well, what it was, anyway. We can head there and see if they made it out. And, if there’s no one there, we’ll see what we can get from what’s left.”

The trio headed East toward Mine 29 with faint hopes that there were survivors. The ten-minute trip was filled with recollections of their own five crew members who were lost when they unknowingly looked into the eyes of the devil that struck their land, along with those on the mine property who couldn’t escape its wrath.

As the truck crept closer to the property, the heart-wrenching destruction came into view. Everything that wasn't made of sturdy materials like steel or concrete was mangled beyond recognition. Deformed pieces of metal littered the ground, scattered around the conveyor belts and coal car fillers, resembling an assortment of twisted bread-ties on a kitchen counter.

""No one on the surface could have survived this. Looks like the same mess we survived by the skin of our teeth," TJ quietly said, shaking his head in horrific amazement.

"We were lucky, TJ. Maybe there were some who were in the mine, same as we were, who made it out. I know where it is, but judging by all this carnage, we will have to park and walk to it. Can't risk getting a flat in all this jagged debris," Dale said in a somber tone.

They departed the truck, grabbing their helmets and mining lights and making sure to lock it to keep any hidden opportunists from gaining easy access. TJ pulled a ragged tarp over the fuel cans to avoid losing the spoils of Flick's hard work. Traversing the terrain was difficult, but the group approached the mine entrance after a few minutes of challenged walking.

"The opening looks intact. Only a few fallen rocks here and there, but it looks sound around the supports. I'll head back as far as I can go and see if it looks like it fell anywhere," Dale stated, as he began to make his way underground. "Not sure it could have avoided falling in."

"Wouldn't go in there if I were you," a tired, gravelly voice said from a distance.

The group froze in place, as Dale whipped his head around to scan their surroundings to see where the sound came from. "Who's there? Friendlies here, checking for survivors."

"You're lookin' at 'em," an older man's voice said, as two men stepped from behind an overturned coal-truck. The man who spoke brandished a sawed-off shotgun, as the younger of the two wielded a pry bar. "And, who might you good-Sams be?"

"Name's Dale Rogers. My friends here are TJ and Flick. We are from #25 up the road and were underground when the world went to hell. Mine collapsed, and we barely clawed our way out. You two inside when it hit?", Dale inquired, trying to find common ground to avoid any triggers that might make the one on the shotgun get fidgety.

"Yep. We were about a mile in. Rest of our crew didn't make it. Big fall behind us took 'em all out. We lost a lot of good people. I'm Red Fleming, and my partner here is Jerome Gray...goes by Speedy," Red wearily explained.

"You folks lose people too? How have you been making it?" Jerome asked.

Dale spoke for the group and said, "We got resourceful and used some of the equipment to help us get free. Powered a drill off the mantrip battery and dug our way out. We lost half our ten-man crew from the big blast. Picked up Miss Flick here after we got my old truck up and runnin'. We've been able to get some food and other supplies from what's left of the stores and other places. You?"

Red spoke up, "Only thing that has saved us is the Stop-N-Go mart on the other side of the property at the entrance. It's block, but it took a hell of a lick. We've been able to ration the food between us, but it's about gone. Water too. We thought you might be lookin' to take the rest of it, if you'd found it on your way out."

"We've been trying to find good people in our travels. Venture a little further out each time. TJ mentioned this mine and that there might be survivors like us, so we had to come and check. Like I said, we found Flick, who has been a big help. We fought off a big crew that tried to take what we had and they've not been back, but we expect 'em to regroup and lick their wounds after they bury the ones that didn't fare so well. We are tryin' to make the mine our home, into a bunker of sorts," Dale explained. "We've been looking to add to our numbers. Any plans?"

Speedy answered before Red could speak, "Absolutely! I'm so tired of pickled bologna and pork 'n' beans. That store must have gotten a surplus buy on those. My blood type is Bean Negative!"

Flick cackled at Jerome's description, adding, "Oh my, I needed that laugh. Not at your expense, but that is the funniest thing I've heard in weeks!"

Red shook his head with a tired grin. "Kid has no sense. Needs to go on the road with that comedy show he's working on." With a pause and a deep breath, he added, "As far as your offer, I was beginning to wonder what was next for us. Haven't seen a soul since we walked out of that opening once we thought it was safe and saw what you see here, except for what was left of the ones who had no warning walking around that morning. We buried nearly a dozen in shallow graves. No working vehicles on the property. That store was our saving grace. Until you folks came along. Just let us know how we can contribute."

"Well then, it's settled," TJ exclaimed. "I'm sorry what you guys went through, but we'd be glad to have you."

Before we head back, is there anything we can use here? We've patched up some of the equipment that wasn't buried using pieces from other things we've run across. 'Frankensteined' them, if I remember Rex's term correctly. Not pretty, but they work."

"Rex who? Used to work with a fella named Rex during the first part of my career," Rex inquired. "Can't be the same one. He'd have to be as crazy as I am for sticking around all this time."

"Rex Walker. He'd be close to your age," Dale answered. "I've worked with him around 12 years, I'd say."

"Yeah! Walker...that was his last name! We called him T-Rex because he's a tall drink of water but had shorter arms!" Red exclaimed. "We all had nicknames. That's how I got mine. Used to have fire red hair in my younger days. Not as fitting now. As far as stuff to use, pretty much everything outside that mine was wiped off the map. All that's left is scrap metal, or it's been burned or blown apart by that nuke."

"Similar situation at 25, too," Dale disclosed. "There were a couple of block office buildings still halfway standing, and we picked them dry of any food, water, first aid, or light batteries. We were lucky to find what we did. No one survived outside the mine. They had to be trying to hit the most productive mines with those bombs to destroy all they did in this region. Who knows how far the devastation spread since we don't have any phones or access to news stations anymore. We've all wondered about our families that live away from here, like my three boys."

"Can't imagine anyone would have survived what hit us. There might be less-damaged places 50 miles or so from here, but how any one lived through it I'll never understand. Like the group you said who hit your place...how did they not die like everybody else?", Red wondered aloud.

"Best I can figure is whoever was in a block basement or tucked into a mountain side away from the blast stood a better chance than anyone else," Dale surmised. "Might have lost all they had, but probably were able to live through it. I'd say the survivors of those situations are the ones who banded together to form gangs in search of better shelter and whatever food they can snatch up. Speakin' of, we probably oughta get goin'. Who knows when that bunch or the next one in line will try to hit us again. Don't want Rex and Sam to fight 'em without us."

"Let's roll out, boys," said Flick. "We just might have us a community comin' together, " as they began climbing into Dale's truck. "I know one thing we need to find before long: deodorant. Y'all are one ripe bunch!"

"You ain't lyin'! I thought it was just ol' Red all this time! Wooo-weee! This crew cab ain't gonna be the same after this trip," Speedy quipped with a big laugh.

"Shut yer yap, Jerome. You don't exactly have rose petals flyin' outta yer ass, you know," Red said with an aggravated tone, all the while as his eyes wrinkled with a grin.

"Uh, oh, Red's pissed at me! He always calls me by my name when I've ticked him off," Speedy said followed by a hearty cackle.

Dale dropped the truck in Drive and rolled towards the mine entrance. "Want me to stop and get some pickled bologna and beans for the trip, fellas?"

In unison, Red and Speedy replied, "NO!!!"

Chapter 9
Coming Together

Each step Dale took was accompanied by the sound of gravel beneath his boots, the only sound in Mine 25. His headlamp cut through the darkness, revealing the rough stone walls that enclose their world. The air was heavy with staleness and a musty smell, reminding him of the dampness and age of this place.

"Be careful over here," Dale warned, his voice echoing off the walls as he pointed to a section where the ceiling looked unstable. They had used timber braces to reinforce it and prevent a collapse; this area was their safe haven now, and they had to defend it like a fortress. The group followed closely behind, their shadows flickering against the walls in an eerie dance. Three new faces joined them, still bearing the haunted expression of those who had witnessed the world's downfall. But in this underground refuge, they were slowly learning to trust again, to find hope amidst the chaos.

"T-Rex, remember when we rigged up that old continuous miner to keep going without a pilot?" Red's voice broke through the silence. He was talking to Rex, recounting tales from days long past.

Rex chuckled from deep within his chest. "That thing ran better without us than with us."

Dale listened to them reminisce, their voices a testament to the resilience of the human spirit. These men had spent their lives digging into the guts of the earth, extracting its riches. Now, they poured that same resilience and expertise into securing a life underground after the world above had betrayed them.

"Air quality's next on the list," Dale said, outlining the task ahead. They needed to ensure that their new home didn't become their tomb. Dale had spent enough time beneath the surface to respect the delicate balance between life and suffocation.

"Got some ideas for that," Rex replied. "We'll need to set up some kind of ventilation system."

"Used to do that back in Mine 29," added Red. "Ain't no stranger to making sure we got good airflow."

"Good," Dale affirmed, nodding. Their collective knowledge was their lifeline, each man's history contributing to their continued existence.

"Feels like old times, doesn't it, T-Rex?" Red said, pausing to wipe the sweat from his face.

"Except now we're mining for our lives, not just coal," Dale replied in a solemn tone.

"Always been about survival, Dale," Rex said. "Just now, the stakes are higher."

They shared a silent moment of understanding before resuming their duties, both aware of the seriousness of their situation. This mine was more than just a shelter; it was their safe haven in this barren and unforgiving new world. They would do everything in their power to protect it.

Dale followed the sun's path as it fought against the thick haze that hung in the sky. He stood at the entrance of the mine, staring out at the solar panels that lay scattered on the ground before him resembling a puzzle of survival and progress. The collection was a mis-match of shapes, brands, and configurations, all of which had been gathered from here and there on their supply runs in hopes they would be useful as an energy source in a world that was on slow time.

"Angle 'em towards the sun's peak trajectory," Dale instructed. "We need every watt we can scrounge."

The group worked carefully and intently, arranging the recovered panels on the rocky ledge beside their underground home. Wires stretched out like veins across the rugged terrain, connecting back to the core of the mine where darkness had its firm grip.

"Light's just the beginning," Flick muttered as she attempted to straighten out a tangle of cables. "But it's a damn good start."

"Fans next," Dale reminded them, his gaze never leaving the task at hand. "Without ventilation, this home will become our tomb ."

As he spoke, the sound of metal scraping against stone echoed throughout the dark and desolate void behind them. It was a necessary move for survival as they worked to mount the fans and bring fresh air into the stagnant space below. Every action was carefully planned and executed.

Below ground, the air was thick with the scent of earth and coal dust. Dale led the way into one of the off-shoot corridors, the beam from his flashlight cutting through the darkness. Here, away from the touch of wind and sun, another kind of growth was imagined.

"See here?" Flick said, her voice echoing slightly off the damp walls. "Perfect for mushrooms. Just need the spores and a little patience."

"Patience we got," one of the men grunted, unloading bags of hydroponic materials onto the rough-hewn floor.

"Vegetables, too," Dale added, assessing the space with a critical eye. "Gotta eat something other than canned goods if we're going to stay healthy."

Under Flick's guidance, they began assembling the makeshift grow beds, piecing together the future from scraps and shadows. Pipes and pumps took shape, a promise of eventual green in front of the gray.

"Never thought I'd turn farmer," Dale confessed, working alongside Flick as they spread the necessary elements.

"None of us did," she replied, halfway giving a smile. "But if we don't adapt, we die. Simple as that."

Their tedious labor continued, steady and determined. Every seed sown, every light fixed, every fan switched on was an act of defiance, a declaration of defiance to the darkness surrounding them.

"Here goes nothin'," Dale whispered, more to himself than anyone else, "under the world we once knew, planting seeds for the world we don't."

Dale trudged through the dimly lit corridor, feeling the heavy air around him. The shallow stream that wound its way through the mine's depths was a potential source of life in their underground home. The sound of water brushing against stone echoed throughout the tunnels, a reminder of the earth's hidden sources beneath the surface.

"Got a thought on this stream," Perry broke the silence, his voice echoing off the stone walls. He pointed to the water coursing steadily beside them. "We can rig up some kinda hydro-power setup. Keep the fans and filters running even if we get cloud cover for days."

Dale paused, considering the proposition. Perry's Marine-trained mind often saw potential where others saw problems. "Could work," Dale admitted, nodding slowly. "But it's gotta be solid. Fans stop, air goes bad... we're done for."

A flicker of pride crossed Perry's face at the validation. "I'll make it solid," he assured. "Won't be my first tango with improvisation."

As they moved deeper into the mine, the light from the helmet lamps found the remnants of the old safety system—a box full of oxygen and methane level meters, their faces dusty but intact.

"Lookie here," Red called out, wiping grime from a meter with his sleeve. "These might still have some life in 'em."

"Let's hope so," Rex added, examining another device. "Don't fancy breathing in anything that could blow us sky-high or choke us out."

"Get them set up," Dale ordered, his eyes scanning the group. "Every corridor, every chamber. If these levels spike, I want to know yesterday."

The team scattered in different directions, each clutching their meters as if they were shields against the unseen dangers that lurked in the stagnant air. Dale watched them, feeling a heavy weight of responsibility. This was not just a battle for survival; it was a constant struggle against an invisible adversary that lurked in the shadows of the tunnels they now called their home.

He knew the dangers that lie ahead, the trials that would test their resolve. But as he gazed at the makeshift community taking shape around him, forged from necessity and bound by shared purpose, a fierce determination settled deep within his bones.

Dale came upon a crosscut left untouched by coal extraction. The air was cool, a stark contrast to the sweat that had collected beneath his clothes from the day's never-ending workload. "Here," he said, "we set up the first aid station."

The group gathered around several worn wooden tables recovered from the surface that were now covered with medical supplies. Boxes of gauze, rolls of bandages, and bottles of disinfectant were arranged in rows, a small pharmacy salvaged from the ruins.

"Red, document what we have," Dale instructed, knowing inventory would be as crucial as the supplies themselves.

Red nodded, "You got it, Dale," as his pen began jotting down the supplies and the numbers of each.

"Good." Dale surveyed the setup, imagining the potential wounds and ailments that would find their way here. Injuries were inevitable; they needed to be prepared.

"Next is the pantry," he said, motioning for part of the group to follow.

As they ventured further into the mine, the light from the entrance faded away as the darkness closed in. A vast cavern appeared before them, once a site of hard labor but now transformed for their survival. Make-shift shelves lined the walls, built with whatever scraps of metal and wood could be salvaged, ready to hold their supplies.

"Spread it out," Dale directed. "Equal distance between supplies. We can't afford waste if something spoils or gets contaminated."

Several group members nodded in agreement, hands moving to organize cans and dry goods with a methodical precision born from necessity. They had gotten into a rhythm that made the process speed along.

"Rex, you got that secondary location figured out?" Dale asked without turning, knowing the older miner would be within earshot.

"Sure do," Rex replied, stepping out from the shadow, his height and build a reassuring presence. "Follow me."

They walked past the pantry, the stream's gurgle a constant companion, until the path veered off, leading them to a forgotten passage. Rex stopped here, pointing to a section of the wall that seemed no different than any other.

"Behind this," he said, tapping the stone with his knuckle. "Hollowed out an extra spot. Only a few know. We'll keep it that way."

"Smart," Dale said, nodding once. "How much can it hold?"

"Enough to give us a fighting chance if we're cut off from the main stash, " Rex shared in confidence.

"Let's hope it never comes to that," Dale said.

"Hope's cheap," Rex countered. "Preparation's priceless."

"Get it stocked. Quietly," Dale added, and Rex nodded, slipping away almost ninja-like.

Dale stayed put, staring at the concealed cache. It was more than hidden supplies; it was a testament to their will to survive. They would not be taken unaware again. Not by starvation, not by invaders. This bunker was their one and only hope for survival and they needed to put every detail into place.

Dale surveyed the cavernous expanse of the offshoot corridor, a flashlight beam cutting through the darkness toward a cleared space. Sleeping bags, once vibrant rolls on a shelf, now dulled by dust and time, were laid in precise rows, each one a barrier against the cold earth of the underground.

"Looks good," he called over his shoulder. The group silently watched for his approval. The sleeping bags had been acquired through scavenging at a sporting goods store, a reminder of simpler times when opting for adventure was a luxury rather than a survival tactic.

"Let's set up a partition here," Dale directed, marking a line with his boot across the gritty floor. "Women's quarters on this side. We need privacy, but keep it close. Safety in numbers."

"Big D's right," a voice said, and Dale turned to see Perry approaching, his Marine Corps bearing unmistakable even in miner's garb. He handed Dale a tattered curtain they'd found among the ruins. "This'll do for a divider."

Dale and Perry worked in tandem, hanging the makeshift curtain with wire scavenged from a past civilization. It was crude, but it would serve its purpose. As they stepped back to appraise their handiwork, Perry nodded toward the mine's entrance.

"Perimeter's next," he said with determination. "We can't have what happened last time happen again."

"Agreed," Dale replied, his thoughts drifting to that night when their security had been breached and the fragility of their sanctuary had been painfully exposed.

Together, they walked the perimeter of their refuge, flashlights dancing over the rocky walls. Perry pointed out potential weak spots, his military training evident in the strategic placement of his fingers.

"Warning system," Dale mused aloud. "Tripwires, cans... anything that makes noise. We rig them up around these choke points."

"Got plenty of wire," Perry offered, pulling a spool from his belt. "And rocks to spare for the vantage points. I can start on the tripwires now."

"Make sure it's subtle," Dale instructed. "We don't want to give away our defenses to anyone or anything prowling around out there."

"Subtle as a fox," Perry assured him, a confident grin flashing momentarily.

"Good." Dale clapped him on the shoulder. "With any luck, it'll be enough to keep us safe."

Dale returned inside and observed Rex's precise movements in the dark mine tunnels. The aging miner used scavenged materials to protect them, and his deliberate actions displayed his mastery of their underground home.

"Careful there," Rex murmured to himself, securing a tripwire at ankle height between two protruding rocks. "A misstep here could be your last."

"Rex," Dale called out, his voice steady but low, wary of carrying down the wrong tunnel. "How are we looking?"

"Like a fortress, if I do say so myself," Rex answered without looking up. "Got deadfalls set up along the east corridor, snares down by the water. No one's getting in here without us knowing."

"Used to be that we'd prepare against collapses and bad air," Rex continued, tying off the end of a wire, "Now it's raiders and whatever else is out there." He shook his head. "Times change, huh?"

"Too much," Dale agreed.

"Speaking of," Rex said as he stood clearing the dirt from his knees, "I've rigged up something special for the main entrance. A welcome mat, you might say."

"Let's hope it's one we never have to use," Dale replied, though he knew hope was a luxury they could scarcely afford.

Rex nodded, a silent acknowledgment of the harsh truth. Together, they navigated back through the maze of traps and defenses, their path marked only by the soft hum of ventilation fans and the intermittent flicker from solar-powered lights.

"Alright, everyone," Dale announced to the group, his voice carrying a quiet authority. "Get some rest. Tomorrow, we fortify the west wing."

And as they disappeared to their sleeping quarters, each person carried with them the knowledge that their safety lay in the hands of the traps laid by an old miner, the watchful eyes of their leaders, and the strength of their newfound family. The night settled in as Dale remained vigilant, listening for the slightest disturbance that would signal their defenses had been breached.

Chapter 10
The Test

With his trained eye, Dale Rogers scanned the jagged edges of the barren Appalachian Mountains that stretched out before him. The sun had set behind the peaks, leaving behind long shadows that reached across the bleak terrain. The air was crisp and smelled of pine, mixed with a hint of smoke from distant fires that were now mere embers.

"Keep it tight," Dale murmured to Perry, who nodded in silent understanding as they led their small party through the ruins of what once was a bustling town. The silence was broken only by the crunch of boots on rubble and the occasional distant echo of a structure giving way to the elements and neglect.

Amid the burnt remains of buildings, Dale noticed a group of people huddled together. His hand reflexively reached for the Colt in his waistband, feeling the familiar steel against his palm for reassurance. As they got closer, the survivors lifted their heads, their expressions were a mix of both hope and fear.

"Who are you?" asked a woman with a knit cap pulled low over her ears and a threadbare shawl around her shoulders.

"The good guys," Dale replied, his voice steady. "We've got a place. Safe. Fortified. We're looking for those willing to work, to contribute to making a community."

The ragged band of survivors talked quietly among themselves, and soon a few brave individuals stepped forward. Their faces showed the exhaustion and fear that came from living in constant danger. One by one, they introduced themselves and revealed what little remained of their former lives.

"Razor's been here," a man with a grizzled beard and a limp said wearily, motioning towards a nearby wall. The red spray painted symbol—a crude blade dripping with blood—was still fresh enough to smell the all-too-familiar odor. "Claims he's kingpin of Appalachia now," the man continued, his voice rough like gravel. "Been takin' what he wants, hurtin' those who stand in his way."

Dale sighed as he considered the implications. Perry's hand tightened into a fist, the scar across his knuckles whitening with the strain. "Appreciate the heads-up. All the more reason for your group to leave this place for one that's better equipped to fight off this new world's evil," Dale said, his mind already racing with plans and contingencies. He exchanged a look with Perry, a silent agreement passing between them. They would take these people back to Mine 25, offer them shelter and hope. But they also knew a storm was brewing on the horizon, one led by this Razor character's ruthless reputation.

"Let's move out," Dale ordered. The survivors gathered their meager belongings, and together, they began the trek to the truck that would lead this weary group to the bunker mine that Dale and his group had turned into a stronghold.

As they walked back into the mine, the sun began to tuck itself in behind the mountains. Dale's thoughts lingered on the painted warning. It was clear now; the one they called Razor was the newest scourge in this post-apocalyptic world, one that might require a harsh response. But first, they would need to fortify their numbers and prepare—not for if, but for when—they would meet this Razor and his merry band. In the new world order, it wasn't just about surviving—it was about protecting what was theirs.

When the newest members entered the bunker, Dale introduced them to the group, who had been collectively hard at work. "Almost didn't recognize the place," he said with a grin, as he noticed numerous improvements since they'd left. "If someone could show our new family members around and make them feel at home."

"I'll do it," Sam said with excitement as she hopped up from her make-shift chair.

"I'll help ya," TJ added, as he shook hands with a couple of them.

"Let's get them situated and fed, and then we will have a group meeting to discuss some new intel we gathered from 'em. Looks to be a potential issue on the horizon that we need to prepare for," Dale said matter-of-factly, as he stroked his graying beard in thought.

The following morning, Dale, Flick, and TJ drove out to a part of the area they hadn't crossed off their map. They typically tried to limit each excursion to a maximum of 15 minutes one way before they agreed to turn around. This location was just on the outskirts of that 15 minute mark, where TJ thought he recalled seeing some truck garages and coal machinery repair shops in the city limits of what used to be Dorton. The intention was to recover welding equipment and check for generators.

Dale did his best not to stumble over the scattered debris leading up to the once vibrant truck garage that was now a hollow shell. The building's ribs were exposed to the unforgiving sky. He scanned the dim interior, trying to determine what lurked in the shadows that could mean salvation or another dead end.

"Over here!" Flick's voice echoed. She stood beside two bulky forms shrouded in dust and cobwebs, as her small wiry frame looked even more diminutive next to them.

"An El Camino," Dale noted, nodding with approval as he ran a hand over the sleek curve of the '76 classic. "And a bus too. Looks like someone was in the process of making it into a camper."

"EMP-proof," Flick said, brushing her red hair out of her eyes. "Old beauties like these will be our lifeline."

Dale watched as she worked with skilled fingers, as most of her freckles became smeared with grease. The El Camino roared to life first, a throaty sound that seemed too good to be true. Then the school bus, its engine grumbling awake after an indefinite of silence during the makeover that had begun to transform it into a camper. "Check 'em over from front to back and underneath to see if you can spot any glaring issues, Flick. If either of 'em need anything, surely we can find it here or close by," Dale said with hope. "TJ and I will load up what we can find in the mean time."

TJ and Dale scoured the garage, salvaging cans of food, bottles of water, and tools that gleamed with promise. The MIG welder they located looked to be in great shape, considering what all they had to pull off of it. Once Flick gave the OK for the makeshift camper, they began loading equipment and supplies into the back.

As day bled into dusk, they gently drove the vehicles back to Mine 25, their newfound resources rattling in the back. The mood was one of victory, but it was short-lived.

The next day, Dale led a small party out again, this time for reconnaissance. They crawled along the ridge overlooking a neighboring town, where Razor's gang had left their bloody signature on the side of what remained of the old high school gym. Buildings were gutted, smoke curled from their blackened frames.

"Disgusting animals," Perry spat, his knuckles white around the binoculars.

"Let's get to work," Dale said with determination. Using scraps of iron plates scavenged from the mine, they fortified their newfound vehicles. Each strike of the hammer against metal was a vow: they would not fall easily.

Flick moved with purpose, welding plates over windows, radiators, and wheel wells. "Won't win any beauty contests," she muttered, "but it'll keep bullets out."

"Function over form," Dale agreed, watching as the last plate was secured to the rear of the bus.

"Big D," someone called out, and Dale turned to see Speedy, one of their lookouts, gesturing urgently. He climbed to the vantage point, squinting down at the valley. Even from this distance, he could make out a group moving methodically from building to building.

"Razor's scouts," Dale concluded, his voice low.

"Or worse," Perry added.

"Keep an eye on them," Dale instructed. "We need to know their numbers, their movements. Knowledge will be our power."

"Understood," the lookout affirmed as Dale descended the slope.

Back at the camp, the mood was somber. They understood the stakes now more than ever. With each new addition to their growing family, their reasons to fight multiplied. Dale Rogers, with every fiber of his being, knew that the real battle for their Appalachian stronghold was just beginning.

The following morning, Dale's gaze followed Sam and Speedy as they disappeared into the twilight with their newest recruit, Stu Osborne, a scrappy young man who'd emerged from the latest group they had given refuge. There was a sincereness to him that had earned Dale's cautious approval; he never suspected the serpent that lay coiled beneath the surface.

"Keep sharp," Dale called after them, "and remember, no unnecessary risks."

"Got it, Dale!" Sam's voice echoed back, her silhouette fading off into the foggy shroud that enveloped the area.

The morning seemed endless, and a blanket of stillness covered the mine where the community had sought refuge. Despite the calm, Dale couldn't shake off an uneasy feeling in his stomach. To distract himself, he checked the perimeter, running his hands along the makeshift barriers made of scrap iron. These rough fortifications stood as a symbol of their unwavering determination to survive.

When the group returned that evening with a bus full of supplies, they were met by Dale and Perry. Speedy was first to depart the bus, and discreetly asked to speak with Dale away from the group. He then spoke of how the new recruit had volunteered to scout ahead in a dilapidated convenience store. When they told him they should do it as a group, he insisted and hurried off almost in a jog, then disappeared briefly. They waited, then searched the building, and were about to give up when they found Stu walking back from the other end of the street. When questioned, he simply said he got lost and wound up a couple of streets over before he realized it.

“Somethin’ ain’t right, Big D. I know everybody likes this cat, but anybody else would flip their shit if they got lost like that in this hell-hole world. Dude acted like he was on a mission, then played dumb when we asked him,” Speedy elaborated, in an untrusting tone.

"Damn it," Dale cursed under his breath. Trusting people was always hard for him, but early on, this kid seemed to check all the boxes. Still, when they left out, he wondered why something didn’t seem quite right. “Wonder if he’s a plant by Razor’s bunch to give them intel.”

Perry looked off into the darkness, then said, "I'll never say never, but, I doubt that. He's helped us big time since he's been here. Risked life and limb a time or two, just to get a wire through a tight spot or to scale a rock face to get something up and over it."

"Be the perfect alibi then, wouldn't it? Fit in like a puzzle piece and no one will be the wiser," Dale said in a hushed but pointed tone.

"I guess we shall see then. Just hopin' your gut feeling is wrong, my friend," Perry said quietly, as he headed for his bed.

"Me, too, buddy. Me, too," Dale said in a whisper.

(Four hours earlier)

Stu Osborne's palms were beginning to sweat when he saw his opportunity to do Razor's bidding and get into his good graces. He had been recalling how Razor's number one goon, Hank, had caught him coming from one of the exits of their warehouse as they returned from a supply run a week earlier. Hank wanted to kill him right then and there, but Stu begged for his life, saying he didn't know anyone was using it and he was just looking for food, but the other items in his possession lead to other conclusions. Razor told him the only way he would live is to do whatever he needed, and he needed someone to go join the group at Mine 25 as a spy.

The mine group had been gathering the majority of the supplies and still-useful items from every corner of the area, and word had it they had slaughtered one of the lesser-feared scavenger groups. Razor saw it as a challenge, and Stu had better not fail him if he wanted to live. If he succeeded in getting intel to Razor successfully, he would allow him to live and serve his needs. He had to do well on this mission, or else. This was his chance.

As Speedy and Sam urged him to hold up on his scouting of a building that bore resemblance of a once-prosperous convenience store, but the building had seen safer times. He knew that was the only opportunity to get out of the sight of his new comrades, so he slipped and slid through the store aisles at break-neck pace to gain distance on the two. He knew Speedy was nicknamed such for a reason, and he saw his only chance at losing them was to put some moves on them in a store he'd been inside of many times.

Stu hadn't been in that particular store in years, but he remembered how to get to the opposite entrance once he got his bearings. He ran through a hollowed-out flower shop that was missing its roof and then came within sight of the post office where he had promised Razor he'd leave the intel. He checked to make sure he hadn't been made, then slipped into the former post office, now just a shell of itself.

In the old mail-sorting room, hidden from prying eyes, he etched his betrayal onto a crumpled piece of paper— a crude layout of Mine 25's boundaries and sectors, an estimate of manpower numbers, and their primary patrol routes—important intel that Razor's gang would need to overtake their sanctuary. He hoped the scouts would find it, and that he would rise through the ranks once word got around of what he had done for the betterment of Razor and his #1 goon Hank, who fancied himself as the ultimate lawman in the new world.

In the mean time, he would make up a story about getting lost and ending up on another street. Hopefully they'd buy it and that would be that. He could go back to the bunker and blend in with the rest of the worker bees, until such time that Razor decides to wreak havoc on the mine and attack their fortifications. He would put up a fight for show only, then surrender to Hank and get taken back to the compound without incident. Only then would he truly be treated like the hero he is and receive his spoils.

Two days later, scouts from Razor's militia were combing the surrounding areas for signs of intel left by Stu Osborne. They had named one place in each corner of the region to place the note, so he could always have an option to leave it wherever Dale's groups extended out to.

As the sun crept across the sky, Kenny stumbled upon the message during his routine sweep. His heart pounded with opportunity; this was his chance to rise above the rank and file of Razor's militia. Clutching the note like the Holy Grail, he tucked it into his coat pocket, his mind already savoring the taste of power.

But greed has a way of unmasking itself, and his three fellow gang members—Ricky, Jay, and Patrick— noticed he was very intent upon concealing something from them. They cornered him near an abandoned gas station and asked him to produce what he had hidden.

"Ok, Ok! It's really nothing," Kenny told them that he would, then abruptly pulled a .38 revolver from inside his coat and fired two rounds into Ricky. As Kenny swung the barrel around at the other two, Jay attempted to grab the gun. The two men struggled over the firearm, with several heavy blows being landed by each participant. Patrick lunged in to attempt to grab the gun when it went off in his direction and struck him in the chest. He collapsed in a heap in front of the still-struggling pair. The confrontation was swift and vicious—an entanglement of fists and boots, with the glint of a boot knife mixed in.

"Where is it, Kenny?" Jay demanded, blood spattering his worn leather jacket.

"I don't know what you're talking about! Get off me!!" Kenny's protests were desperate, as his fear was rising.

They didn't believe him. They couldn't afford to.

Jay was able to separate from Kenny and grabbed a nearby 2x6 board. He wheeled around, and with one swiping blow across his right cheek, Kenny went down. Several panicked overhead blows ended the threat. He pulled his semi-automatic pistol from his rear waistband and fired three wild shots into him, just for good measure. His hands shook as he retrieved the bloodstained message, the weight of his actions heavy on his conscience. To make sure there were no witnesses, Jay fired two more rounds into Ricky, who already lay motionless on the ground.

But survival in the post-apocalypse left no room for remorse. Jay worked quickly, arranging the bodies, crafting his alibi with meticulous care. By the time he limped into Razor's compound, the story of his harrowing escape was etched deep into his expression, ready to be unfurled before Razor's skeptical eyes.

Chapter 11
Razor's Quest

The old warehouse was filled with an uncommon silence while most of Razor's gang was out on their supply runs. Razor sat on a makeshift throne made of scavenged car seats and rusted metal, speaking to Hank who stood nearby, leaned back against a wall with his arms crossed.

"Damn lucky, Hank," Razor proclaimed, tracing the scar on his face absently. "If we hadn't been passed out cold in this godforsaken pit, we'd be ash."

"Fortune favors the passed-out, boss," Hank replied, his big voice rumbling through the large building. His long black ponytail swayed as he shook his head with a grin.

"Before all hell broke loose, I was another soul snatched up by the mines, like so many others around here. I think I made out pretty well, considering, trying to make a living out of the fencing business." Razor said as he started off. "Now, we take what we want."

"Same here," Hank added. "I enforced laws that never did right by me. Now, I basically am the law here. We can establish our domain, no matter the cost."

Their conversation was abruptly interrupted by the sound of heavy boots pounding against concrete. Hank swiveled around just in time to see Jay, one of the scouts, stumbling back into their fortress alone, a stark contrast to the group of four that had set out together. The guards at the door followed behind him, their faces reflecting both admiration and shock.

"Jay's back, brought somethin' from Stu, the rat you sent into Mine 25," one guard announced.

"Well isn't that somethin', now?" Hank eyed Jay skeptically, noting the lack of usual bravado in his posture.

"Got the intel, didn't I?" Jay panted, brandishing a bloody and crumpled letter.

"Let's hear how you managed that." Hank's suspicion was evident as he escorted Jay toward Razor.

With each step, Jay felt the air seemingly growing thicker as he mentally rehashed his story. Hank watched Jay squirm under Razor's piercing gaze as he recounted his tale.

"Snuck up on 'em. Just grabbed it and ran," Jay said, but the quiver of his voice said otherwise.

"Is that so?" Hank prodded, circling Jay like a shark. "Because knowing you, I'd say you stumbled upon it, or worse...which might be the reason you are the only one of four to come back. And those others seem like they have more dog in them than I've seen in you."

"Well, I fought 'em off too, if you want to know the truth. A big group of their folks saw us and yelled, and when we didn't stop, they started shooting like wildfire. The other three boys got hit and didn't make it," Jay explained....pausing uncomfortably before telling more of the story. "Two of their guys attacked me and I fought like hell. Took them out. Then shot two more as I made my run for it. I circled back and grabbed the letter from that post office, then high-tailed it outta there."

"Damn, Jay. I didn't realize we had a Jason Bourne in our midst, but props to you, buddy. I need to learn some of your moves," quipped Hank, his tone oozing with sarcasm.

"Enough!" Razor's command sliced through the tension. He snatched the letter from Jay's grasp. "We've got what we need."

Hank looked at Jay and rolled his eyes as he shook his head. “Get outta here, hero. Go clean yourself up.” Hank then studied Razor's face, seeing the new direction of focus in his eyes, and knew that despite the inconsistencies in Jay's story, the gears of Razor's mind were already turning, plotting their next move to expand their kingdom in the ashes of the old world.

Hank's fingers traced the lines of the Mine 25 compound, sketched onto the crumpled piece of blood-spattered paper. The drawing was primitive but sufficient to stir his tactical instincts. He looked up at Razor, whose eyes were fixed on the plan with predatory interest.

"Seems like they've got a cozy little setup," Razor mused. "Those mine corridors would be perfect for storing our growing stash. We're bursting at the seams here."

"Yup," Hank agreed. "We'll need a solid strategy. They won't just roll over."

"Get your crew ready," Razor ordered. “We need to make sure they are prepared to do whatever it takes.”

With a sharp whistle, Hank called the members of his gang to assemble in the dimly lit warehouse. The group was a diverse mix of individuals, united by their shared struggle to survive in this world. The glow from the improvised lanterns cast eerie shadows on their faces, some showing eagerness while others remained fearful of the mission ahead.

"Listen up!" Hank barked. "We're divvying up into squads. If you have a military background, step forward."

A handful of men and women shuffled out from the group, their postures subtly different, carrying hints of discipline rarely seen by the new world around them.

"Good. You're now leaders." Hank's gaze swept over them. "The rest of you—you're grunts until proven otherwise. We have work to do."

"Boot camp starts now," he bellowed, leaving no room for arguments. "You'll learn to follow orders, to fight without flinching, to not piss your pants when the bullets fly. You ultimately serve Razor. That's a privilege. Sacrifices will be made, but your names will echo in the halls we're about to claim."

They nodded, some with determination, others masking the unrelenting grip of fear. Razor watched from the shadows, his presence an unspoken threat and promise combined.

"First lesson," Hank continued, his eyes laser focused. "Stay alive. Second—make sure the other guy doesn't."

As they broke off into groups, Hank heard the familiar sounds of weapons being checked, along with the echoes of voices reciting orders. Even though the atmosphere was tense and uneasy, there was an underlying sense of determination and grit. This was not just about staying alive; it was an opportunity to take charge and change their rough existence into one of strength and authority.

"Mine 25 won't know what hit 'em," Razor growled as he looked over his makeshift army.

"Let's make sure of that," Hank replied, with the weight of responsibility settling on his shoulders as he oversaw the preparations. Each member of the gang had a role, and he would quickly mold them into the force needed to conquer, to thrive in a world where mercy was a memory and sheer force was the enforcer of the only law they acknowledged.

Their destiny was unclear, a twisted road through toxic forests and abandoned towns. But with Razor's drive and Hank's leadership, they were determined to create a new empire from the ruins, regardless of the sacrifices along the way.

Dale's heavy boots compacted the gravel of the perimeter as he continued his evening patrol. His gaze scanned over the rugged shape of the Appalachian ridges, cast in a fiery red glow from the setting sun. It was a prophetic sign for what was to come at some point in the near future, be it tonight or tomorrow. The rumors were spreading that Razor's militia was on the move, and they could be closing in on them at any moment.

"Big D," TJ called out, jerking a thumb over his shoulder toward the mine's mouth, "Stu's at it again."

Dale nodded, his expression unreadable. He'd known Stu just long enough to anticipate his habits, but recently, something had shifted. Stu's constant desire to explore beyond their borders, as well as the questions that begged of details too precisely at their defenses, didn't sit right with Dale.

"Keep loading those supplies," Dale instructed TJ, then set off towards Stu with a long, quick stride born of track and field decades ago.

Stu was perched on a rock-covered embankment, binoculars in hand, scanning the tree-line. He immediately became uneasy as Dale approached, the subtle sign of a man caught in a mental conundrum.

"Seen anything?" Dale asked in a flat tone.

"Quiet so far," Stu replied, lowering the binoculars.

Dale stood beside Stu and looked out at the same stretch of wilderness. "You've been pushing for more runs outside, asking about our weak spots. You looking for something in particular, Stu?"

"Precautions, Dale. Can't be too careful." Stu's answer came quick, almost too rehearsed.

"Careful is good," Dale said slowly, turning to give Stu a hard look. "Makes me wonder why you're the only one sounding alarms we ain't heard yet."

"We all want to protect this place, don't we?", Stu asked, failing in his attempt to look shocked and puzzled.

Dale immediately noticed the unspoken words in the tightness of Stu's jaw and the constant movement of his eyes. He didn't need to hear it from anyone else; his intuition told him what he didn't want to admit. Stu was a liability, and if they didn't fix it, they could all go down with him.

"Let's head back," Dale suggested, clapping a firm hand on Stu's shoulder. "We need all hands for the supply tally. And Stu..." Dale's grip tightened just slightly. "Stay close."

As they walked back to the mine's entrance, Dale felt the weight of command heavier than ever. Their sanctuary, a maze of tunnels and hard-earned resources, was under threat—not just from the outside but within. The dwindling supplies were a puzzle he could solve with rationing and strategy. Betrayal, however, was a poison with no antidote.

"Everything alright, Dale?" Flick asked as they passed through the makeshift gate.

"Keep your eyes open tonight," Dale said, the seriousness in his tone leaving no room for doubt. "And trust your instincts. If something feels off, it probably is."

Flick nodded, understanding the gravity of the order.

Inside, the mine was buzzing with activity—everyone moving with purpose, their faces carrying lines of worry and determination. They were a family, bound not by blood but by the mutual desire to survive in a world gone mad with power and loss.

Dale surveyed the scene before him, knowing that when the time came, each person would play their part in defending their home. Tomorrow was a gamble, the next hour a mystery, but for now, they had the mine.

Dale walked back and forth along the perimeter, taking in the weary expressions of his group members as they returned from their assigned tasks, both on the grounds and outside this safe haven. They were all exhausted, their protective gear stained with the dirt and debris of a land ravaged by nuclear devastation. The once lush greenery of the Appalachian mountains now lay lifeless in shades of dreary gray and charcoal, serving as a harsh reminder of the bleak future they were forced to pursue.

"Rogers!" Perry's voice cut through the air like a knife, urgent and edged with suspicion. Dale turned to see the younger man gripping Stu's arm, his stance rigid with military precision.

"Easy, Perry," Dale ordered. He needed to handle this personally; Perry's grip could be as crushing as his interrogations.

"Dale, this rat's been sniffing around, asking questions only a scout for Razor's thugs would need to know," Perry fumed.

Dale approached, his gaze locking onto Stu's deceptive eyes. "Continuing our earlier conversation, Stu, what exactly have you been up to?" he asked, his voice low and firm. A leader had to be a pillar in times of chaos and uncertainty, and Dale's presence was as solid as there was.

"Nothing, Dale, I swear!" Stu stammered, trying to wriggle free from Perry's iron grip. "Just trying to help, is all."

"Help? By mapping out our defenses in your head? Razor put you up to this?" Dale pressed, closing the distance until he shared the same troubled air with Stu.

"Look, it ain't like that," Stu protested, but the tremor in his voice betrayed him. The signs were there, clear as day to a seasoned veteran like Dale—Stu was hiding something.

"Then explain," Dale said, his patience wearing paper thin.

"Okay, okay!" Stu's resistance crumbled under the weight of Dale's stare. "I was just checking if we're ready, that's all! You know, for when they come!"

"Who's 'they'?" Perry interjected pointedly.

"Victor, er—Razor's—men," Stu confessed in a deflated tone. "But I didn't tell them nothing, I swear on my mama's grave! I just know they want this mine, and there's a lot of 'em, and they're loyal to Razor and his number one guy—Hank...he's an ex-cop, and thinks he's the law in these parts now. He helped 'em rack up on weapons at the old police department that had the guns stored in a room that didn't get wiped out."

“Is that so...they plant you in that town to get you into our group?” Dale asked.

“Y-Yeah, Razor heard your group was a bunch of do-gooders who tried to add survivors to your numbers and he figured it was just a matter of time before you got to them and offered them sanctuary. I came in a few days before your group found 'em and told ‘em I lost my family. Th-they took me in,” Stu confessed.

"Enough. That just makes me sick," said Dale, as he silenced Stu with a raised hand, his mind racing with the implications. If Stu had indeed leaked information, their entire strategy would need reevaluation.

"Perry, kindly take him to the common area. We'll keep an eye on him until we figure out what the truth is," Dale ordered. “Beginning to think that kid wouldn’t know it if he fell in it.” Trust was a rare commodity these days, and betrayal could not be taken lightly, especially with so many lives at stake.

While Perry forcefully pulled Stu away, Dale remained vigilant over their sanctuary. This mine served not only as a refuge from chaos, but also as a testament to their determination and resilience; it was their stronghold against the approaching evil.

The crisp mountain air carried a chill as the sun dipped below the mountain tops, casting long shadows across the compound. Dale knew the night would bring no rest. In the heart of Appalachian mine country, they had to remain vigilant to survive.

Dale relied on the flickering lantern light to illuminate the crude table covered with scattered maps and hastily written notes - a patchwork of hope and resilience. He had to formulate a new plan that would catch Razor's goons by surprise; maybe by going on the offensive instead of waiting to be hit, they could neutralize being outnumbered.

Dale then returned his focus to Stu. "Exile is not an option," Dale stated, his voice echoing off the damp walls. "That'd be too good for him. Stu knows too much. If Razor's boys get their hands on him again, they'll bleed him dry of every scrap of intel."

Perry nodded. "We keep him here then, under lock and key. He spills nothing more. Pretty sure I've heard of that Hank guy. He got into a bunch of trouble a few years back as a deputy and had to quit. Big dude, from what I remember. It was in all the papers about him being on the take, and he just barely escaped a bunch of charges of brutality to his arrestees and prisoners by resigning."

“Sounds like a real upstanding guy, that Hank,” Dale said with a sarcastic inflection. "It also sounds like that Razor guy and Hank are meant for each other in this hell-hole world.”

"Agreed," Perry said. “Regardless, we need to come up with a plan and a contingency plan, too,” as he leaned over the map of the mine property.

The group focused on strategy and survival. Dale leaned closer to the map, tracing routes with his finger. "They outnumber us, that's a known fact. But we've got home field advantage, regardless of what Stu leaked to them. And, thanks to Stu, we know how they're thinking, and we can flip the script on them."

"Like a passive-aggressive ambush, so to speak," Perry mused aloud. "Hit 'em where they least expect it, on their paths into the property before they even go eyes-on. Rex found some explosives stored up in the remains of one of the buildings on the property, and I can make some wicked stuff with it. We can take the fight to them before they even reach the mine, since they probably think we'll be sleepin' in."

"Exactly." Dale said with a firm but deliberate nod. "We've got choke points they don't know about. You can set some traps on the trails. And if they make it this far, Rex can turn these tunnels into a maze of traps they won't walk out of."

"Let's get to work then," Perry replied, the group rallying around the two leaders.

Meanwhile, miles from the mine's deceptive sanctuary, Hank shaped his own forces. Under the cloak of darkness, his group assembled like specters among the ruins of what once was a peaceful mountain town.

"Listen up!" Hank yelled, commanding their attention. "Razor wants Mine 25, and we're going to give it to him. We move at first light, quick and fierce. No mercy will be given."

His words were met with nods and nervous bursts of agreement as weapons were checked and packs were shouldered. Each person knew the role they played in Razor's grand scheme and each was ready to spill blood for their leader's quest for beginning a new empire.

Back in the mine, Dale surveyed his crew. "This ain't gonna be a walk in the park," he admitted, barely above a whisper. "But this is our sanctuary, and I'll be damned before I let a bunch of ruthless animals and thugs march in here and take all we've worked for."

"Absolutely," Perry added. "We nearly died in this mine once already, and I don't plan on tempting fate again. We will be the tone-setters for this war. They want what we've got. But they ain't gonna like what they get."

"Damn straight!!" the crew echoed, their voices merging into one unified chorus that filled the mine from beginning to end.

As the darkness settled around them, both sides readied themselves for the inevitable confrontation, understanding that by sunrise, whatever new normal they had come to know would no longer exist. In the midst of a barren post-apocalyptic world in the Appalachian mountains, two groups geared up to battle for an uncertain future, relying only on their collective intelligence and determination to forge onward and into the next stage of their existence.

Chapter 12
The Reckoning

Dale crouched down and carefully surveyed his surroundings. He could see the traps they had spent countless hours crafting from scraps of their former comfortable life, all set up and ready to go, thanks to Perry's expertise. Most were hidden beneath layers of fallen leaves and scattered debris. Any step out of line, and Razor's thugs would find themselves tangled in snares or impaled on sharpened stakes.

The individuals surrounding him were a diverse group, made up of former miners and townspeople. They were all on edge but resolute, fully aware of the consequences if they failed.

As the light of dawn crept over the outline of the barren mountain backdrop, Dale felt a cold shiver run down his spine. It wasn't fear, but a chilling resolve. He knew without a doubt Razor and his right hand man, Hank, would appear at any time and outnumber them with five or ten times the manpower.

His rag-tag group was clad in the equipment they'd found at the sporting goods store and other random locations. Nearly every member had some form of protective helmet that had been repurposed from football, baseball, and hockey. Although they were nowhere near the level of military-grade ballistic helmets, they afforded their users protection from most blunt force trauma attacks to the head and face that they'd likely encounter in close-quarters hand-to-hand combat. And they were better than nothing against everything else. The rest of the equipment—bats made of metal and wood—were utilized as striking weapons, as Perry instructed them how to use them with efficiency and force.

Weeks earlier, Perry had found a case of spray paint in an abandoned hardware store and made a command decision to cover all the reds, blues, greens, and yellows of the equipment with the less than vibrant shade of black primer. This way his group looked more like a fighting unit than a high school all-star showcase.

Speedy held his repurposed football helmet and looked upon it fondly as he put it on. "Brings back old times. I used to do some damage back in my day. Makes me feel like ...Madder Max ...with this black helmet and visor."

Dale didn't want to jump the gun and have his troops play a long waiting game, as that would mentally exhaust them quicker than it would physically. However, he couldn't chance the group getting caught by surprise, either. Weighing these options with deep thought, he ultimately made his choice; with a quick hand gesture, he motioned for his snipers to take their positions along the high ground of the mountain above the mine and atop what remained standing of the coal tipple, its iron and steel support structure bent and twisted as if it were an aluminum can. The snipers were the first line of defense, and their aim had to be impeccable.

Other members were placed strategically throughout the rail yard, where they could use the overturned coal cars as cover. When the area was struck, the cars were scattered about like a model train set kicked by an angry little brother.

Perry crouched in the shadows of the dilapidated office building, feeling the weight of his AR-15 from the sling around his neck, and his fingers feeling for the reassuring outline of his boot knife. He could sense the enemy's presence approaching, a primal instinct ingrained in him after surviving in this wasteland. Each leader had their own counterpart, and it seemed that Perry and Hank unknowingly were fated to face each other. Both were leaders with a ruthless and forceful nature that emerged when provoked. Perry had suppressed his brutal tendencies and instincts after returning to post-war civilian life, but this world had brought them back to the surface.

Hank found he was able to establish a reputation early on and then throughout his brief law enforcement career, with a tendency of beating down suspects and those who dared dismiss him when he had them in custody. It didn't take long for him to adopt this behavior as his preferred treatment for everyone he came across who didn't see things his way, especially those he shook down. He knew in today's battle that he must be prepared to fight for his life, while also leading his mishmash bunch into battle with the hope that numbers alone could be the deciding factor. He felt he had prepared them for what they were about to face. Hank did not want to fail Razor.

As Hank's assembled forces disembarked from two of Razor's old roll-back flat bed trucks, he looked over the group, confident he had trained them to put up a fight against the outnumbered foes. "Form up!" Hank's voice bellowed out over the foggy terrain that surrounded them. "We will march through the old town of Dorton, where Jay found the intel. This will give us a direct route into their mine entrance, where we will spread out and hit the trails Stu so graciously mapped out for us."

Jay's stomach dropped. He knew he'd staged the scene of his battle with the three other scouts to look like they'd been attacked by the enemy, but his best hope would be if wildlife had found the remains and feasted on them, to hide any screw-ups he didn't think of in such a rush.

As the formation passed by the old Post Office, Hank barked out, "HALT!", and the group quickly stopped. Jay swallowed hard, almost as if he'd had a golf ball lodged in his throat. "Where was this letter you found? If Stu used this location, he had specific instructions where to leave it. You scouts were supposed to know where it was hidden," Hank disclosed with a glare that cut through the fog like a laser.

"Well, uh... it was right where he was supposed to leave it. Good ol' Stu!" Jay stammered .

Hank's glare was unwavering as he asked, "And where was that? Refresh my memory."

"Uh...well I ran in so quick, it's hard to remember exactly where, because we could hear the enemy comin'," Stu replied, hardly convincing in his explanation.

"Alrighty, Jay. Well I'm sure you were in 'beast-mode' after that, mowing down the enemy and all," Hank said with a grin that didn't reach his eyes. "But, where are our fallen comrades you said were killed by the those who were after you?"

"W-Well, they were right...over there....I mean, we...were over there," Jay stuttered. Hank walked to where Jay's uncertain pointed finger directed him and looked around, picking up shell casings, looking at bloody clothing that was strewn throughout the small area.

"Looks like fortune has shined upon you on this foggy morning, since the animals have taken care of this battle ground," Hank said in an unconvincing monotone, as he compared several identical shell casings in his palm by flashlight. "But, since you are the hero among us, I appoint you the leader of this group of rabid dogs. You will be the tip of the spear for this operation into the lion's den. Maybe there will be a statue of you one day, Jay." Hank turned to the group, then returned his focus to Jay with a stare, "So, lead them."

Jay's eyes widened as he realized he was as good as dead if he didn't come through now. He walked to the front of the group and held his right arm up high, then nervously yelled, "Let's move out!", shaking, as he began the two mile march in low-light conditions to their target area.

The anti-ambush began with a deafening boom as one of the traps was sprung. Dale's heart pounded in his chest, adrenaline surging through his veins. He peered through the scope on his rifle, scanning the chaos below. A lone figure in a battered green and white football jersey emerged from the trees.

Jay burst through the opening with a badly injured right leg, waving his arms frantically, rallying his fellow troops forward. Razor had sent him ahead to prove his heroism on the biggest stage, the battlefield. In Jay's haste to push forward and lead the group, he stepped right into one of Perry's shallow spike pits. Stifling a scream from the pain, he quickly recovered, wanting to set an example for the others. Jay appeared from the tree line and right into Dale's sights.

"I've got him," Dale muttered to himself, lining up the crosshairs between the 3 and the 7 on the man's chest. He took a deep breath, exhaled halfway, and pulled the trigger. The shot rang out, echoing through the valley like a death knell. The man in the football jersey crumpled to the ground, and chaos erupted below.

As the militia swarmed the choke points, they were met with a barrage of gunfire and Perry's homemade traps. Improvised spikes, tripwires, and even a few well-placed hunting traps wreaked havoc on Razor's forces. The woods echoed with the sounds of gunfire, shouts, and screams, but Dale's focus never wavered. He picked off the militiamen one by one, dropping them with his scoped rifle before they could reach the entrance to their sanctuary.

"Keep 'em pinned!" Dale's voice barked through echoes of varying calibers of firearms. But Perry's gaze was already locked on a larger figure barreling through the melee—Hank.

"Ah, THAT has to be Razor's pet. He's mine," Perry muttered, more to himself than anyone else. He slung his rifle, drawing the knife from his boot. With a fierce determination, he charged toward Hank, meeting him head-on in a violent clash. The two men were titans, each move calculated, each strike meant to be lethal. Blade clanged against blade, and their fists blurred in rapid exchanges. Perry's training in Krav Maga and Jiujitsu met Hank's brute force head-on, neither giving an inch. "Come on, you son of a—" Perry grunted, narrowly dodging a knife thrust aimed at his ribs. He countered with a swift elbow to Hank's jaw, but the bigger man hardly flinched. They grappled, bodies twisting in a deadly dance, each seeking an opening, an advantage over the other.

Both sides' fighters carefully avoided the two engaged in their own personal war, knowing it was a battle to be reckoned with. While smaller skirmishes raged on, they paled in comparison to the heavyweight showdown between the alpha-males intent on determining who truly ruled this battlefield.

Nearby, Speedy found himself disarmed, wrestling with a thug who had managed to close the distance, unseen from his blind-side, and knocked his long gun to the ground. Speedy wheeled and grabbed the man's shoulders with his powerful hands and landed a sharp knee to the gut, which sent the thug reeling, but Speedy wasn't done. He brought a loose rock across the man's face, jarring his opponent back onto his heels. Speedy then sprinted towards him like a running back through the hole on 4th and Goal, smashing the front of his helmet into the man's temple and hearing the crunch that left no doubt. He landed next to the man, but quickly gathered himself with his head on a swivel, just in time to see Sam in danger.

"Sam, behind you!!" Speedy's shout cut through the noise. Sam turned just in time to deflect a blow with the butt of her rifle, then swung it like a club, knocking her attacker to the ground. She instinctively sent a front kick into her attacker's face and dropped to a knee, instantly following with lightning-quick punches and a sharp elbow to his head. She retrieved her rifle and followed with two rounds to made quick work of that situation, her extensive MMA training setting the tone for anyone who witnessed.

"Hold your ground!" Dale's voice roared above the noise. But even as he barked orders, he couldn't tear his eyes from Perry and Hank.The fight had become a brutal test of endurance, both men bleeding, both refusing to fall. The other battles that surrounded the two participants gave them their space, as both sides knew this one was pivotal.

Hank unleashed a relentless flurry of blows to Perry's back and kidneys while he had the former Marine down to a knee. "You boys think you'd just get to keep your cozy place from me?", Hank spat out between strikes. Perry gritted his teeth with each connection, then timed it perfectly to cause the big man to miss and lose his balance. Perry then took advantage of his chance—Hank's stance faltered for a split second.

"Damn right, big boy,", Perry growled with pain in his tone as he summoned every ounce of strength and drove his boot knife deep into Hank's side. Hank's eyes widened in shock and pain before he crumpled to the ground.

Perry quickly jumped into position to place a guillotine choke on his sizable adversary. "Well, you failed, Roscoe, " Perry said as he bent down to Hank's ear. "Boss Hogg ain't gonna be happy." Perry clamped down with all his remaining strength until he was sure Hank would not get back up.

"One down," Perry panted, sliding his leg from beneath his lifeless opponent and yanking his knife free.. But there was no time to celebrate. Razor's wave was upon them, a relentless surge of bodies pushing Dale's crew back.

"Here they come!" Dale called out as he eyed his scope, "And it looks like Razor is leading 'em." The sanctuary was under siege, and the fight was far from over. The scent of gunpowder and blood filled the air as the militia pressed forward, overwhelming the defenders with sheer numbers. "Fall back!" Dale commanded, gripping his rifle tightly. As they retreated, the sounds of combat echoed through the mine's tunnels.

TJ rose from a tightly packed rock formation near the entrance to lay down cover fire for those stragglers trying to get inside the mine. Razor spotted him and raised his heavy .44 Magnum, firing several shots toward TJ, striking the rocks and sending fragments into TJ's face, temporarily blinding him. Several other members of Razor's group fired upon the mine entrance, to which Perry responded with his AR-15, as he emptied a full magazine into the group from an elevated position he'd reached above the mine. His rounds found their marks into a dozen of the assailants, cutting the group into half its previous number. TJ was able to stumble into the mine entrance because of the efforts Perry put forth. After an emergency reload, Perry then made his way inside to join his group.

Razor paused briefly to assess the status of his group, many of whom had dropped during the initial phase of his attack, which was met with a plethora of unexpected traps during their ingress. Numerous injuries were inflicted at the hands of a faceless assailant, but the largest number of fallen had just came at the hands of Perry, who unleashed hell upon them. His face, Razor had burned into his memory. One change of plans beget another, and he fully intended to take the mine from this band of malcontents, but his new focus was on this man who methodically slaughtered so many without blinking an eye. Razor no longer had a visual on Hank, but he had a gut feeling this new threat had something to do with it.

Dale hurried his group into the mine and towards the safety of designated areas he, Rex, and a few others had prepared in case of invasion. "Just keep going," Dale growled, "We have to reach the inner tunnels."

Razor's men poured into the mine like a relentless tide. Dale could hear Razor's voice among them, barking orders, ""Push forward, boys! They can't run forever!"

Each thump of Dale's heart echoed in his ears, a constant reminder of what was on the line. His entire community, his new family—they had all fought to defend this way of life. He caught glimpse of Perry, who now was noticeably limping from an injury at the hands of Hank, yet still stood tall and tried to mask his pain.

"Fall back!" Dale yelled, his voice breaking with sheer desperation. "Just fall back!" "It's too late," Razor taunted, pressing his advantage as he inched closer and closer to victory. Dale stumbled again, the world spinning around him, Razor's blade coming ever closer. And then a shot rang out. Razor staggered, shock replacing his menacing sneer.

"Move, move, move!!", Dale turned and commanded towards the group, his voice bouncing off the rough walls and low ceilings of the mine. The sounds of hurried footsteps and panicked yells filled the air as his crew dashed deeper into the twisting tunnels. Sweat dripped down his face, blurring his vision. He wiped it away with a shaky hand, clutching his rifle tightly in determination.

"D, they're right on us!" Sam's voice was strained, barely audible over the deafening sound of combat. "Just keep going," Dale growled, "We have to reach the inner tunnels." The group met Flick and Red coming out to help, but Dale's emphatic point had them hurriedly turning back the way they came from.

"Rex in place?" he yelled towards Flick and Red, to which they both nodded that he was indeed. "Good, it's almost show time," he said to himself as he tried to keep up his expedited pace.

Razor arrived in sight of the mine entrance with his wave of followers, although he had lost roughly half a dozen along the way. The unsprung traps Perry had set found their marks when Razor's group entered from a different direction than Hank's squad.

"Hurry!" Dale barked, guiding his crew into the depths of the mine. The air became colder and denser, the darkness pressing in on them. They reached a narrow pathway, only big enough for Razor's gang to squeeze through one at a time.

"Set up here," Dale ordered. "Sam, you and TJ cover the entrance. Perry, you're with me."

"Got it," Sam nodded, positioning herself behind a makeshift barricade. TJ crouched beside her, reloading his firearm with shaking hands, trying to fight through the debris still lodged in and around his eyes.

"Steady, TJ," Dale said, placing a reassuring hand on the young man's shoulder. "You've got this."

"Yeah... sure thing, Dale," TJ muttered, trying to settle himself.

The first of Razor's men appeared in the entrance, cautious but determined. Dale responded by sending a burst of gunfire his way. The man dropped, and another took his place. The narrow passage turned into a choke point, exactly as Dale had planned.

"Keep them pinned!" Dale yelled, firing again. The sounds of gunfire and screams filled the tunnel, a symphony of violence and desperation. "Get back to the rendezvous point! Tell Rex we're comin'! That stack of bodies should buy us a minute or two."

"Dale, we've got movement!" Perry called out, pointing towards the choke point. Dale turned, catching sight of Razor himself, effortlessly snatching his lifeless fighters, and those without any fight left in them, off the pile. Within moments, Razor unleashed a small fresh group of militia, as Dale's group retreated into the mine opening.

"Here we go," Dale muttered, bracing himself. He hadn't expected to encounter them so soon into their tactical retreat. He knew Razor's clan had them dead-to-rights before they could reach their next rendezvous point.

Razor's cold gaze met Dale's, a wicked grin spreading across his scarred features as he once again raised his left arm and aimed his deadly .44 Magnum at the foe. "End of the line...Dale, is it?", Razor sneered, stepping forward like a supervillain in a climactic scene. "And there's that sumbitch who mowed down my boys just as we were getting to the party."

"Damn, you really do favor Boss Hogg," Perry responded. "I told your head goon that....Roscoe, was it?... as he was taking his last breath. He thought he was tough, just like you do."

Razor glared at Perry and slowly moved the hand cannon from Dale's direction to Perry's. "Is that right? Looks like we found the tough guy of this merry little band right here," Razor growled, eyes narrowed behind the sights of his gun.

"Ah...a .44 Magnum? Kinda like the guy who drives the big 4x4 to compensate for other issues...am I right?", Perry said pointedly to Razor with a sarcastic grin.

Dale noticed that Razor's attention was solely on Perry, and realized that his comrade was deliberately trying to provoke Razor as a diversion. It was working. While Razor and his men were distracted by Perry's efforts, Dale shifted his stance to his other foot, preparing to strike. He gave a quick glance at the three men at Razor's back, all of whom had lowered their long guns while watching the verbal exchange.

Dale subtly coiled himself as if he were a Jack-in-the-Box. With lightning quickness, he sprung towards Razor in an attempt to get the gun or at least knock it loose. Dale struck Razor's weapon-hand with enough force to free the gun from his grip. The force of the impact caused Razor to stumble backwards, slamming the side of his head into the rocky wall behind him. He slid down the face of the moist surface and fell into a heap on the mine floor.

Dale saw his chance and rolled towards the weapon, snatching it from the ground and, before the men could react, fired at two of the them, striking them both. Perry spun and retrieved his AR-15 from its resting place on the ground and took out the third, then double-tapped the two Dale had winged.

Dale immediately turned to his waiting comrades and yelled down the corridor, "Gamma...Gamma!!", which was the signal for Sam, TJ, and Flick to gather everyone else and continue to the rendezvous point. Rex had designated the alternate passage way for them if Razor's group made it this far.

During the commotion directed at his men, Razor had gotten back to his feet after his bout with the wall had momentarily taken him out of commission. With the force of a linebacker, Razor dove head-first into Dale, who had lowered the pistol while directing his group members to safety. Like two Generals head-to-head on a battlefield, they fought tooth-and-nail for control of the gun.

As Dale felt the unexpected blow from behind him, he was able to quickly compose himself when he and Razor crashed to the ground. Dale's only defense in his predicament was to blindly land a backwards right elbow-strike to Razor's temple while his opponent kept both arms clasped around his left arm and midsection. Razor loosened his grip to attempt to block the continuous elbow feed from Dale, as both realized the devastating effectiveness of each. Realizing he couldn't take many more of them, Razor instinctively tried to tuck his head slightly as he soaked up another one in exchange for quickly taking his protective right arm down and reaching his karambit blade tucked in his back waistband.

"KNIFE!!" Perry screamed, as Dale's eyes immediately widened in an attempt to locate its faint gleam in the dimly lit corridor. In a blur of motion, Razor began wildly swinging the deadly knife around Dale's defensive right arm towards Dale's face and chest. Dale's sheer determination momentarily held off his would-be assailant.

Perry attempted to put Razor in his rifle's cross-hairs and end this attack on his friend. The chaotic struggle between the two combatants left no opportunity for a clear shot. Perry's eyes followed the erratic movement of the knife's glint against its dim backdrop and suddenly lost sight of it over his rifle's sites. Dale's agonizing scream filled the corridor, as Razor plunged his blade into an unseen target. The sound abruptly stopped, indicating Dale was no longer in the two-man battle. Razor's cold thought process instantly had him use Dale as his shield, with an even colder gaze directed at Perry. Razor's left arm darted out from beneath Dale's limp body and retrieved his Magnum, its barrel leveled at Perry.

Perry knew he was a dead man after what he did to the Razor's militia and their recent pointed conversation. "Screw it," Perry muttered to himself. He sprinted towards Razor, hoping to avoid a clear shot since his nemesis was lying at an odd angle on the ground. Instead, he found himself staring right down the ominous barrel, one that for a millisecond he believed he could sling a basketball through and not touch the sides.

"BOOM!!!" The powerful weapon sounded off the rock walls in every direction, as Perry instinctively dropped his head and stopped in mid-run to soak up the round he knew had his name on it. Inexplicably, he felt no pain, and looked up to see the large gun, tumbling aimlessly with a small plume of smoke trailing out of the barrel, like a plane at an airshow. As it clattered onto the ground, Perry immediately looked to the entangled men to see that Dale had somehow thrown himself on top of Razor's arm and the gun, blood pooling from beneath him.

"NOOOO!!!" Perry screamed in vain, knowing the ultimate sacrifice his friend had just made for him and the group.

"Go!! Get everyone...to...Gamma...," Dale struggled to yell, using every ounce of his strength to hold off Razor from getting a second shot at Perry. Razor, who outweighed Dale by nearly a hundred pounds, was struggling to get free from the hero's intense grasp. "Goooo...I've got this."

Perry hesitated and started to run to help his comrade, but the remaining members of Razor's militia were making their way through the choke point after clearing a path through the debris that was courtesy of Rex. Perry looked at Dale and saw the concern in his eyes, then simply nodded. Perry turned to the group members, who were in their own stages of disbelief and anguish, and ushered them further into the labyrinth of the mine and towards the Gamma rendezvous point. He knew Dale gave them time to get away from danger by sacrificing his safety for that of the group.

TJ, Sam, and Flick were almost at Gamma Point when they realized that several members were missing. TJ sent the others ahead and turned back to check on Dale, Perry, and the other members who were no longer behind them in the corridor. When he saw Perry and several familiar faces approaching once again in the dimly lit tunnel, he turned back toward Gamma and yelled, "Rex, Red—fall back to Gamma Point!" TJ's voice cut through the chaos as he barked into the mine corridor, his tone steady despite the dire situation. He could see Rex nodding in understanding, determination etched on the old miner's face.

"Got it!" Rex replied grimly. They had rehearsed this retreat countless times, but now it was no longer just a drill. Their lives were on the line. The group would lead the invaders through a side tunnel that was rigged to collapse at the beginning and end to trap their pursuers inside. Rex had carefully moved large rocks and other debris into the regular corridor to look as if it was impassable.

"Move it! Move it!" Perry urged his crew, motioning for them to follow him. The militia was pouring in through the main tunnel, their sheer numbers pushing Perry and his team back inch by agonizing inch.

"Remember the route," Rex stressed to the group as they ran. "We've got one last trick up our sleeves."

Perry and the group ran through the side tunnel that was cut in a path back to the main corridor. This path was likely intended to get the larger equipment through, but on this occasion, it was affording them a lifesaving opportunity to escape Razor and his mob. The object was to get them to be in pursuit of them through the detour and trap them there.

"Keep moving! Almost there!" Perry encouraged, leading his team deeper into the alternate tunnel and out the far exit. He glanced at Rex beside him, who gave him a brief nod of reassurance before turning his attention back to the approaching militia.

"Tripwire is set!" Red called out from the side passage, expertly timing the trap to slow down their pursuers. "Should give us some room to breathe with the smaller shots startin' 'em off."

Perry felt a heaviness in his heart with each passing moment as he wondered if Dale possibly could have survived. They finally reached the pre-chosen area, past the narrow corridor that Rex had carefully rigged with explosives. It was their last stand.

"Setting the charges," Rex warned. "We'll make them pay for every step." He looked over his detonator unit as he tightened the cables, then quickly looked around. "Wait, where's Dale??" Rex asked as he paused the process of setting off the blast.

Perry glanced at Rex in the dim backdrop, then shook his head before facing the tunnel again. "Stand your ground!" Perry commanded , raising his rifle. "Dammit," Rex muttered to himself.

""Clear!!" Rex hurriedly shouted. Everyone knew that was the signal to tuck in behind cover and shield themselves.

"Incoming! I can hear 'em running through the detour!" Perry shouted, pointing towards the outlines of their opponents against the dim light of the tunnel.

"Now, Rex!" Perry yelled as their enemies closed in on them. And then it happened—the earth shook violently as Rex hit the switch, causing the pre-determined section of the mine to collapse and cutting down a large portion of Razor's forces.

"That'll buy us some time," Rex panted, his face showing both weariness and determination.

"Hopefully so," Perry replied bleakly, taking stock of his dwindling crew. He looked around for everyone who'd come with him and noticed TJ down on a knee beside Flick, both caught up in emotion. Sam wiped her eyes and wheeled around with gritted teeth after she'd checked on them and pointed her rifle towards the carnage unleashed by Rex, then lowered it when she saw no survivors emerging from the dust and fallen debris.

But then she saw it—a glint of metal in the dim light and Razor charging through the debris like a bull possessed.

"Rex, watch out!" Sam screamed, but it was too late. Razor's blade found its target, striking Rex and causing him to crumple to ground, blood pooling beneath him.

"Rex!" Perry cried out, rushing to his side. But it was too late; Rex's eyes were already glazed over as he struggled for breath.

"Perry...finish this..." Rex gasped, weakly gripping onto his arm. And then he was gone.

"No, damn it!" Perry roared in anguish, fueled by rage and sorrow. He turned to face Razor, his own knife drawn and ready for the final showdown.

"Party's over, punk. It's just you and me," Razor sneered as he advanced with deadly intent.

"That's supposed to scare me, Razor?" Perry spat back bitterly, lunging forward to meet his enemy head on. They clashed fiercely, blades flashing and blows landing with brutal force. Despite his exhaustion, Perry knew he must fight with every tool in his mental toolbox, as Razor was a relentless maniac.

"Let's see how tough you really are," Razor hissed, slamming Perry against the wall. Pain exploded in Perry's back, but he pushed through it, swinging a backfist into Razor's jaw. The big man stumbled back, shaking the cobwebs from his head.

"Fall back!" Perry turned and yelled to his friends, his voice breaking with sheer desperation as he thought of Dale's heroic act just moments earlier. "Just fall back!"

"Too late for that," Razor taunted, as he regained his balance, knife gleaming in the dim light of the lanterns hanging beside them. "You brought the wrong boys and girls to the playground. Should've brought some fighters instead of this pitiful bunch."

Razor charged at Perry with the force of a grizzly, slamming him against a massive rock and holding him down with his weight. Perry gasped for air as the impact forced the wind out of him. Razor seized his opportunity, steadily gaining ground and inching closer to victory.

Disoriented, Perry stumbled once more, the world spinning around him. As he tried to shake the cobwebs from his mind, he noticed a pick-axe handle within his reach. Its iron head was nowhere to be found, but it was something at least to keep him in the fight. With a tornadic effort, Perry spun as fast as he was able and struck Razor across his upper arm, knocking him back a step.

Perry again swung at Razor, who was able to lean just out of its path of destruction. As Perry tried to keep his balance after the missed effort, Razor landed a heavy kick to Perry's right knee. Perry dropped to the ground in pain but attempted to get back to his feet. Razor slammed his thick left forearm across Perry's neck and shoulders, stunning him.

Razor raised his blade overhead, preparing to strike the final blow in their ongoing feud. "You've had this coming since the moment I saw your little punk ass," he sneered.

From the depths of the mine a shot rang out as blood instantly covered Perry's face. Razor staggered, shock replacing his menacing sneer. As Razor dropped to a knee, realizing his plan was failing more by the second, he glared back at his unknown adversary . A second shot filled the chasm, as Razor fell onto his face into the coal dust that once surrounded him during the only decent days of his adult life. Perry regained his footing to see the outline of a man, standing there, with a rifle smoking in his hands.

"Stu?? What the hell? How did you..." Perry asked, in disbelief of what had just taken place. He wiped the blood off his face with his sleeve, then grabbed his rifle and double-tapped Razor's unmoving girth to make sure he would never steal another breath from anyone in this mine.

Stu stepped into the lit area and looked around at the shocked group members who appeared mentally and physically spent. "I once read somethin' where a lady said that some of the greatest battles are fought in the silent chambers of your soul. Well, I fought a thousand of 'em in that holding cell," Stu said, as he lowered the rifle.

"How in the world did you get free?", Perry asked, trying to piece together the mental puzzle before him. "And why would you shoot your boss?"

"I guess the blast from that side tunnel knocked the iron slab you'd rigged up off its brace. It tilted to the side and left enough room to crawl out. I heard the commotion when the smaller charges went off, and then pretty much silence after the big boom. I was just trying to catch up with you all when I saw that big maniac fixin' to cut you up. Luckily I'd grabbed a rifle from one of Razor's dead troops once I got out into the main corridor and just happened to get a good shot at him," Stu explained.

"And, to answer your question: I never liked that asshole," Stu continued. "He had me over a barrel and there was never a good ending for me. Razor treated me like a stray dog. You guys took me in, regardless of what my job was, and you treated me like a human being. That meant somethin' to me. This was the least I could've done to gain your trust back and repay you guys. I swore that if I ever got out, I'd make things right with you all for takin' a chance on me.""

"Well you sure made up for it, and then some. Dale always liked you and I took up for you when things weren't adding up," Perry said with gratitude in his tone.

"Speakin' of Dale, I need to thank him, too. He took me with open arms. It crushed me to have to beat around the bush with him," Stu confessed. "Where is he?"

Perry looked down, trying not to well up. "That asshole you took out killed him. Dale saved me, saved our group. Sacrificed himself to get us to the rendezvous point. You avenged him and didn't even know it. I'm very grateful to you for that."

The sound of boots crunching and kicking gravel appeared suddenly from the main tunnel. All hands on deck grabbed their weapons to face whatever foe dared to appear, for this would be the last thing they ever saw. The group was mentally spent and physically battered, but they were always on watch for their home.

An unfamiliar shape emerged into the dim light. Speedy limped into the view of the group, Dale's lifeless figure in his arms. Perry immediately hurried to him to help carry Dale, the hero who deserved the gratitude of every member before him. The two grieving men laid Dale onto the cold earth that he fought so fiercely to protect. Sam covered him with a tarp to give him his dignity in their presence.

"I got shot in the leg outside the mine before the battle moved inside. I used my belt as a tourniquet to help stop the bleeding, but I lost so much, must've passed out. Just came to not long ago. I was tryin' to make my way in to help, thinkin' I could catch them from behind, but I kept findin' bodies. And then I found Dale's," Speedy said, taking his helmet off and wiping tears away as he spoke. "I couldn't believe it. Even though I didn't know him long, he was like a superhero to me. Knew just what to do, always one step ahead. Just a solid, solid human being. I couldn't leave him there. He deserves whatever we can do for him."

Red and TJ walked to where Rex took his final breath after he, too, saved the group with his heroics in the form of explosives and traps to thwart off and eliminate so many of Razor's thugs. Rex was laid beside Dale and covered with the same care and respect.

As grizzled and hardened as the group was mere moments earlier, their immeasurable grief could not be contained in the presence of the two warriors. These men had showed them light in a world of darkness.

"Let's clear the mine and make sure we are safe. Might be others still finding their way back to us," Perry declared. "TJ, come help me. Sam, check Speedy and the others and dress their wounds with the med-kits. Dale and Rex would want us staying focused."

After 45 minutes of checking each side corridor and behind every hiding place, Perry called out, "All clear." There was much work to be done, but first there was time for a moment of reflection.

Red declared, "Rex and Dale were absolute heroes. None of us would still be here without 'em. Godspeed, gentlemen."

Epilogue- *Honoring Legacies*

Perry stood over the two freshly prepared graves and addressed the group members who were gathered for the somber occasion. "Two of our friends--our heroes, our family--are here before us after each made the ultimate sacrifice for us. Dale and Rex asked nothing of us, but gave everything for us. We humbly stand here with immeasurable gratitude, and we pledge to do everything possible to carry on the legacies that have been forged through their dedication and hard work, all for the betterment of this group...this family, and our sanctuary. They set the standard of what it means to have servant hearts. Thank you, gentlemen. This will conclude our ceremony."

TJ walked over to Perry as the group dispersed, "You said it perfectly, Perry. They were heroes. I'm gonna miss both of 'em."

"Yeah, well said, Perry," Sam said as she patted him on the arm. "I still can't believe they are gone."

"I can't either, Sam," Perry said somberly. "This new world has taught us that we can't afford to mourn like we want to, but we will damn sure honor them. We have big shoes to fill, but we have to forge on. We have so much work to do here."

Red added, "Those two wouldn't want us staying sad and mopin' around. They were all about doing what needs to be done. That's how we honor 'em."

"I checked the El Camino and the bus after everything settled down," Flick declared. "Each of 'em took some stray rounds, but the extra shielding we put on protected the main areas, for the most part."

""Good.. We need to do somethin' with all of Razor's crew we dragged out of the mine," Speedy suggested. "That smell is wretched."

TJ added,"Yeah, the ones around the perimeter have mostly been accounted for, but the ones that haven't will draw whatever wildlife is still out there lookin' for a meal. We need to haul those away, too."

"Sounds like an unpleasant start to this new day, but a necessary one. We can't make progress in the other areas when we have those tasks on the back-burner. Let's all just get that part over with, and then clean up anything that is a reminder of what led us to this point," Perry said in a leader's tone. "We need a fresh start."

"Agreed," echoed the group collectively with nods of approval.

"Let's get to it. Then, we can look to build up our family," Sam suggested. "We can let 'em all know about Rex and Dale."

"I'll always tell the new members about Rex's sacrifice to keep what we still have," Red said among them all. "I miss my old buddy."

"Same here, Red," Perry said, staring off at the sun tucking itself in behind the mountains. "Ol' Rex...we argued like brothers. He knew just what buttons to push," he added, shaking his head with a grin.

Red and Sam both laughed and nodded in agreement. "He loved to mess with us!" added Sam.

"I thought the world of Dale. His boys were his light that kept him pushing through hell and high water for all of us," Perry added."Felt like I knew 'em all. He asked me to try to find 'em if anything ever happened to him, and I promised I would," he added, reflecting on many conversations he'd shared over the last few years, but especially since everything changed. "If anything, we owe 'em for that. I want to do all I can to carry on his legacy in this dark world, " he said somberly. "As long as I have a breath, I will always tell Dale's story."

About the Author:

I was raised in the Appalachian Mountains, in the small coal town of Jenkins, KY. My father was a Vietnam Vet in the USAF, then a coal miner for nearly 20 years. My mother is an angel on Earth for raising three rambunctious boys with immeasurable patience and love. I have two children (Lindsay and Peyton), and four bonus children (Brayden, Channing, Joey, and Kaylie) with my amazing wife, Nicole.

I am a proud graduate of Jenkins High School ('88). I attended Union College to play football, then transferred to Morehead State University, where I graduated with a Bachelor of Arts degree. ('92).

I joined the Kentucky State Police in 1993 and worked as a road Trooper for 17 years in different roles. In 2017, after spending the last seven years of my career on the Governor's Security Detail in Frankfort. I have recently returned to law enforcement in the role of School Resource Officer with the Sheriff's Office.

I never seriously considered writing until lately, so hopefully there will be a few of you who want to follow my journey. Thank you for your support!

~DK

Email: DKHall.author@gmail.com.

https://www.amazon.com/stores/author/B0D6844PCT

Made in the USA
Columbia, SC
13 September 2024

095f098d-9bde-4c68-99f7-137d9555c5beR01